STONE ARCH BOOKS
MINNEAPOLIS   SAN DIEGO

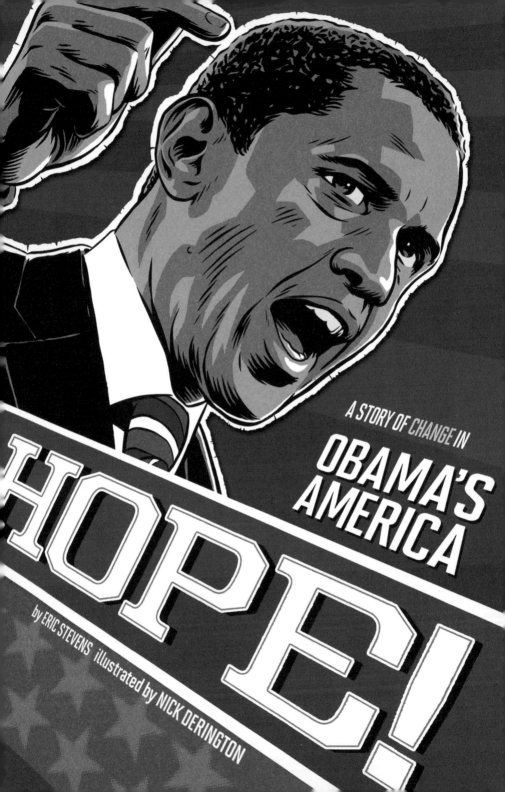

A STORY OF CHANGE IN

OBAMA'S AMERICA

HOPE!

by ERIC STEVENS illustrated by NICK DERINGTON

CONTENTS

DESIGNER: BOB LENTZ   CREATIVE DIRECTOR: HEATHER KINDSETH

EDITOR: BETH BREZENOFF   EDITORIAL DIRECTOR: MICHAEL DAHL

Graphic Flash is published by Stone Arch Books, 151 Good Counsel Drive, P.O. Box 669, Mankato, Minnesota 56002
www.stonearchbooks.com Copyright © 2010 by Stone Arch Books. All rights reserved. No part of this publication may be
reproduced in whole or in part, or stored in a retrieval system, or transmitted in any form or by any means, electronic,
mechanical, photocopying, recording, or otherwise, without written permission of the publisher.

Library of Congress Cataloging-in-Publication Data
Stevens, Eric, 1974-
 Hope! : a story of change in Obama's America / by Eric Stevens ; illustrated by Nick Derington.
   p. cm. — (Graphic flash)
 ISBN 978-1-4342-1724-0 (library binding)
 1. Obama, Barack—Inauguration, 2009—Juvenile fiction. [1. Obama, Barack—Inauguration, 2009—Fiction. 2. African
Americans—Fiction.] I. Derington, Nick, ill. II. Title.
 PZ7.S84443Ho 2010
 [Fic]—dc22   2009013568

Summary: Anton Fox is sentenced to community service and watches the inauguration of Barack Obama.

Printed in the United States of America

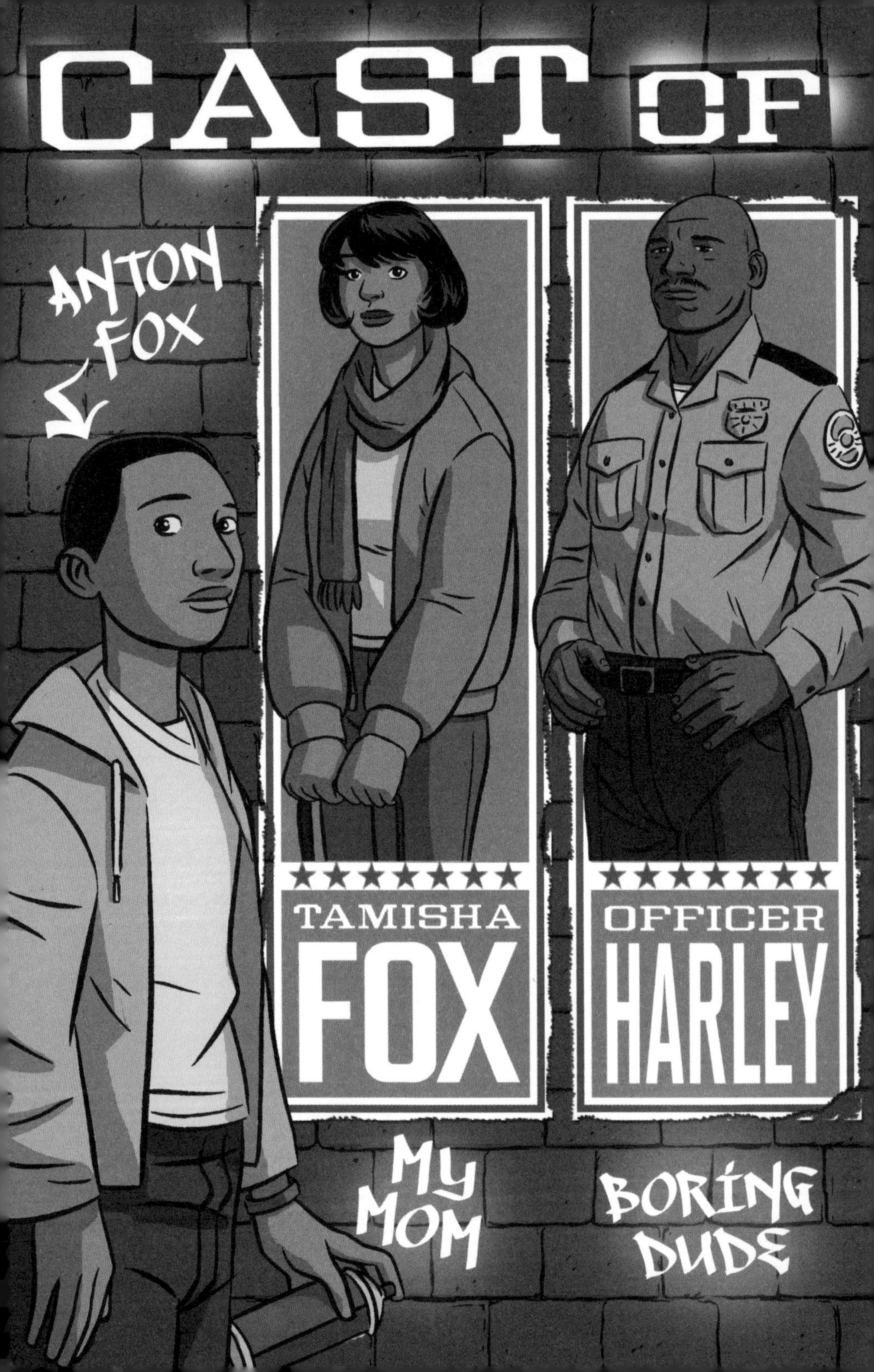
CAST OF
ANTON FOX
TAMISHA FOX
OFFICER HARLEY
MY MOM
BORING DUDE

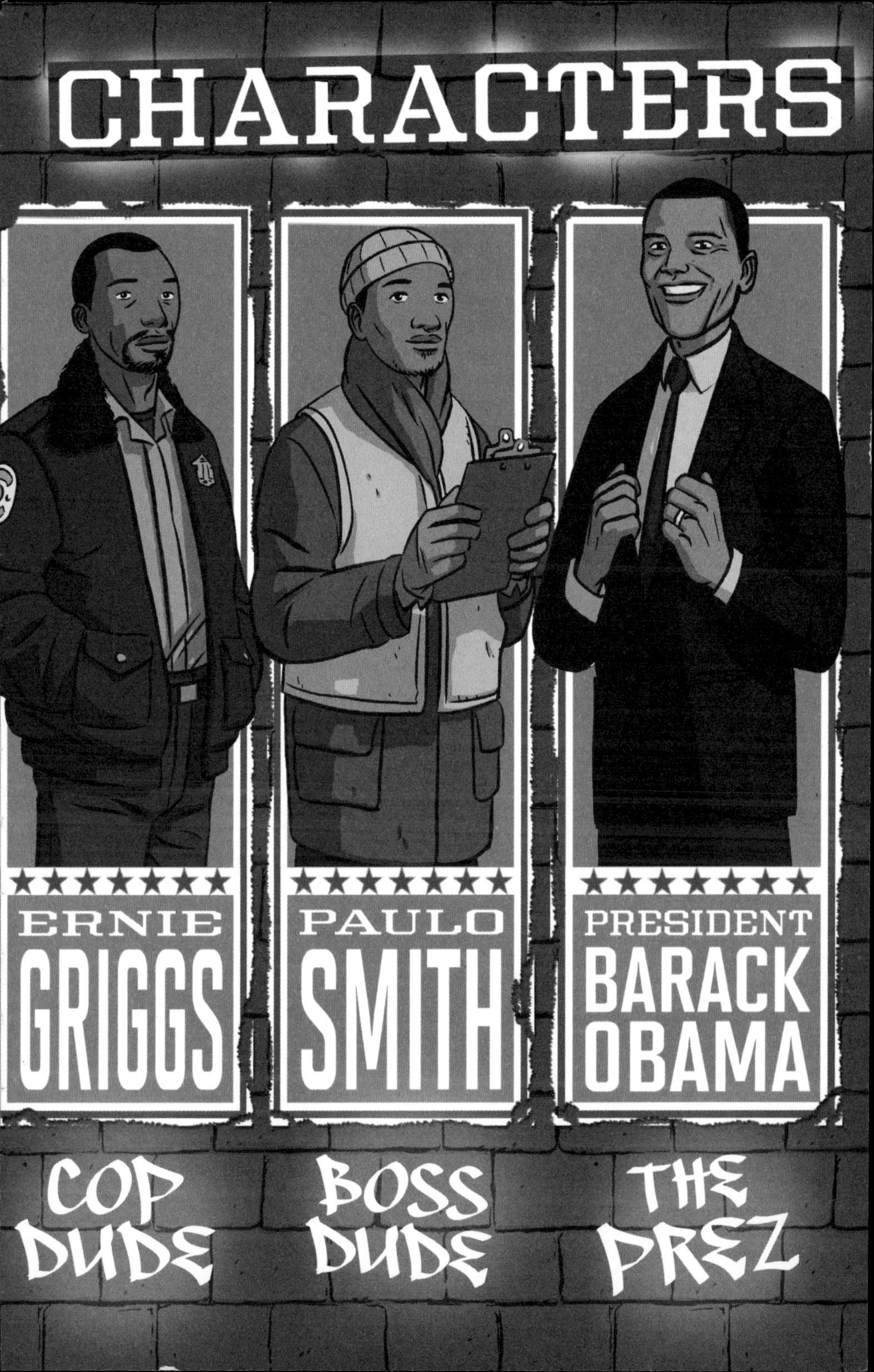
CHARACTERS
ERNIE
GRIGGS
PAULO
SMITH
PRESIDENT
BARACK
OBAMA
COP
DUDE
BOSS
DUDE
THE
PREZ

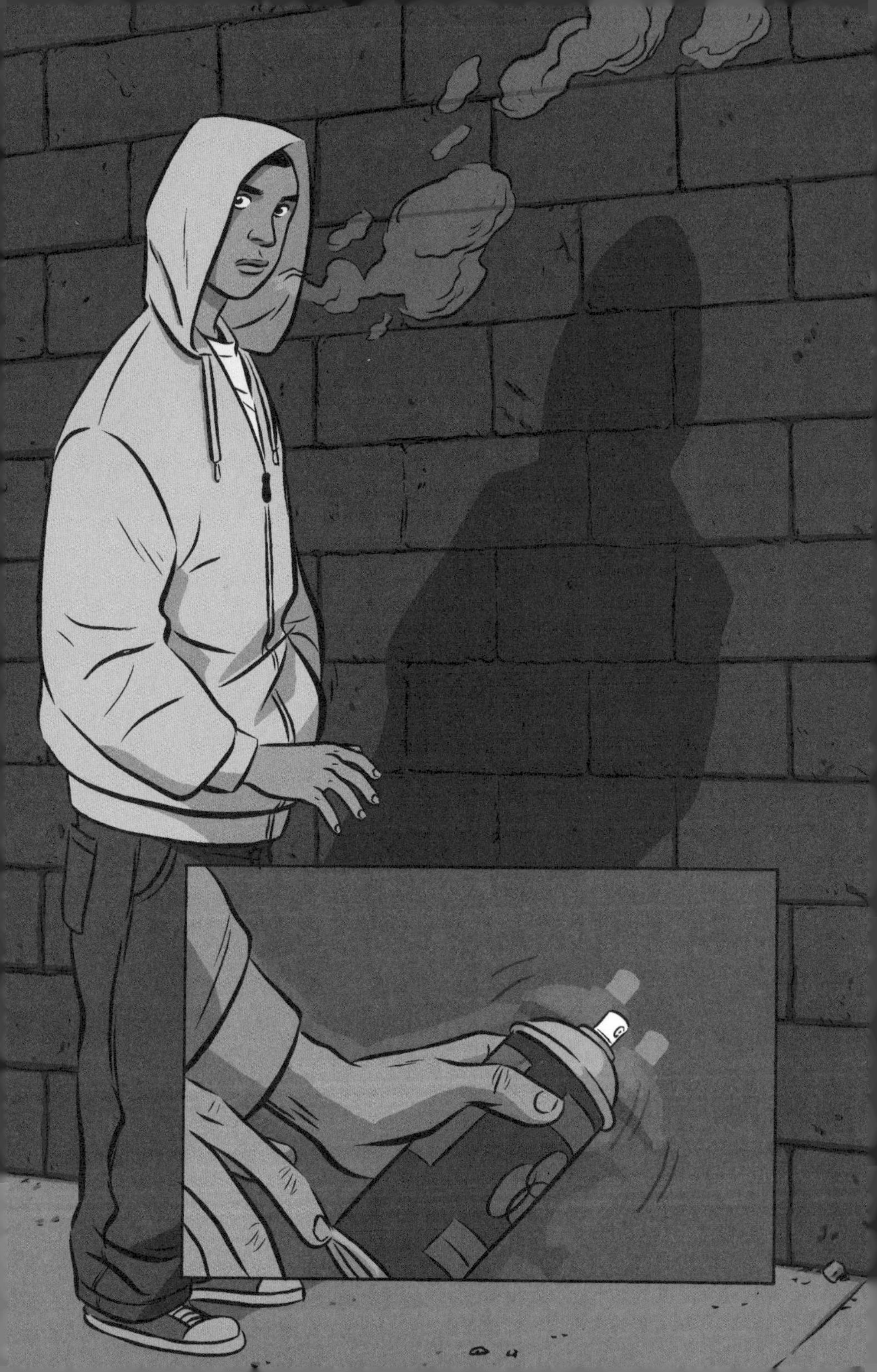

CHAPTER 1

BUSTED

Early on a Saturday morning in January, Anton Fox stood in front of a brick wall, gritting his teeth. Puffs of vapor left his mouth as he breathed into the cold morning air. He stared at the wall, like an artist would stare at a blank canvas, or like a writer would stare at a new sheet of paper. With his right hand, he shook a can of red spray paint.

As he stood there, he thought about the last twenty-four hours. Friday had been a rough day. First, he missed the bus to school. It was a cold and windy morning, especially for Washington, DC, his home city. The walk was long, and by the time he got to homeroom, late, his cheeks were ashen and stung.

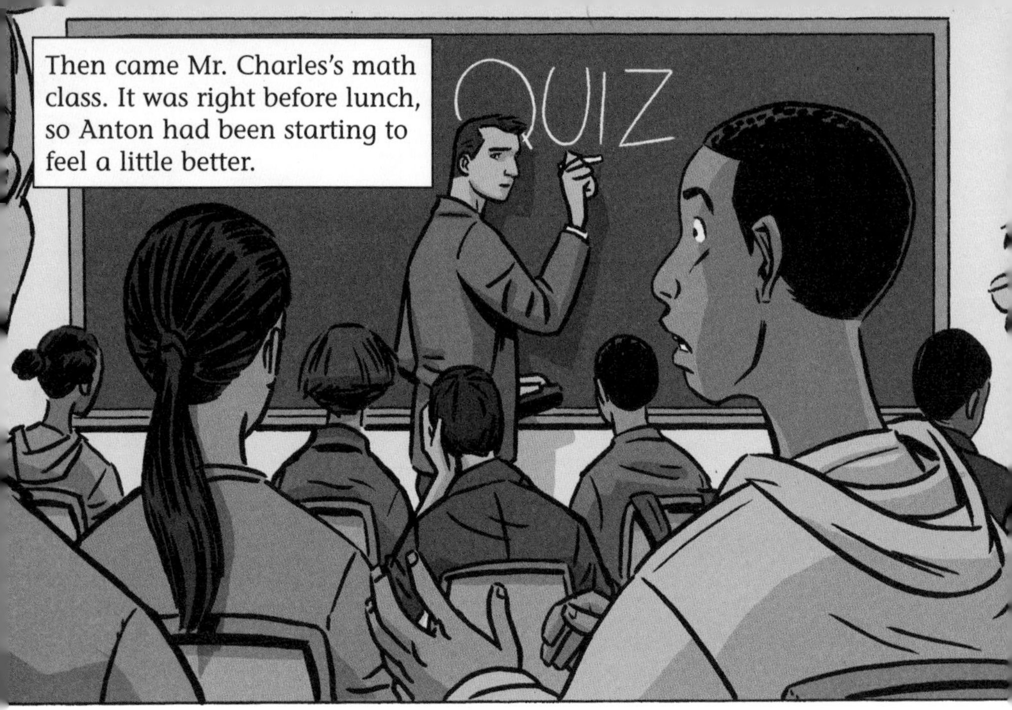
Then came Mr. Charles's math class. It was right before lunch, so Anton had been starting to feel a little better.
QUIZ

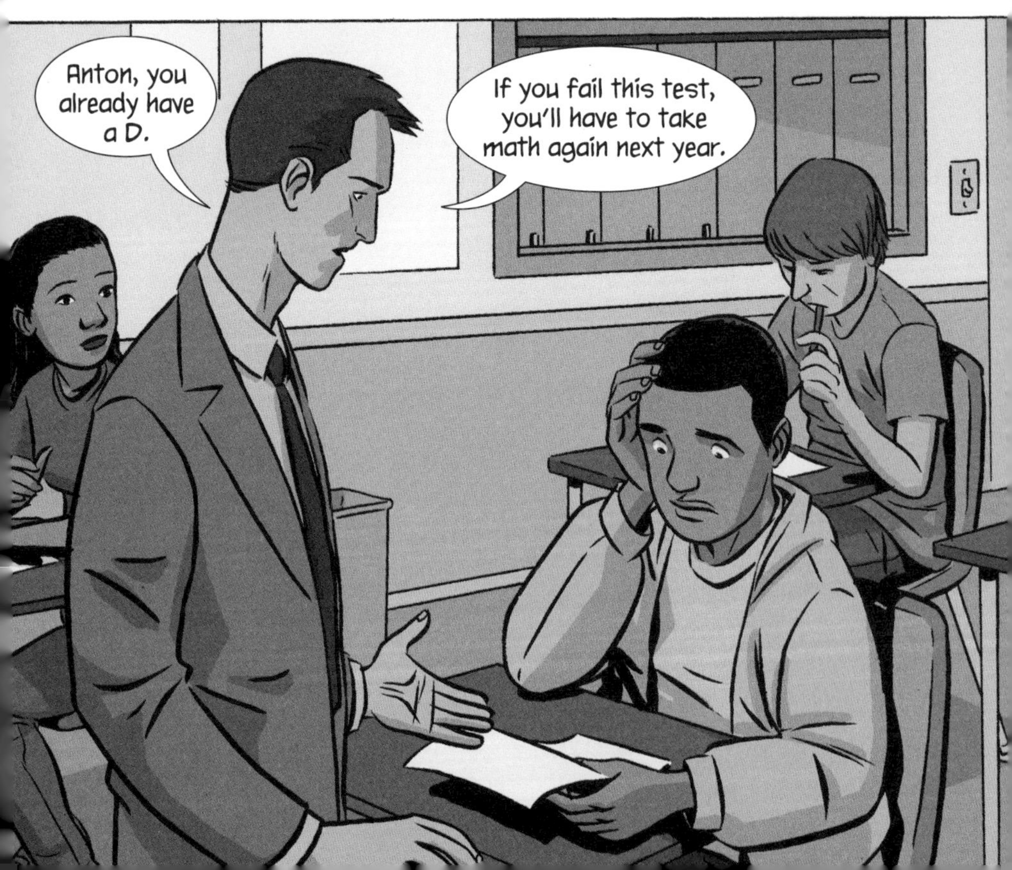
Anton, you already have a D.
If you fail this test, you'll have to take math again next year.

"And that ain't happening," Anton muttered to himself.

He stared at that brick wall. It was the south wall of the high school.

He'd walked all the way down here at the crack of dawn, knowing if he waited too long, even on a Saturday, there'd be too many people around. It wouldn't work. He'd get caught, or he'd lose his nerve.

But here he'd been, standing there for almost an hour. He was angry at Mr. Charles, but he'd never spray painted on a wall before.

This was vandalism. If he got caught, he might get in serious trouble.

Anton shrugged and gave the can of paint one last good shake.

Then he raised it up.

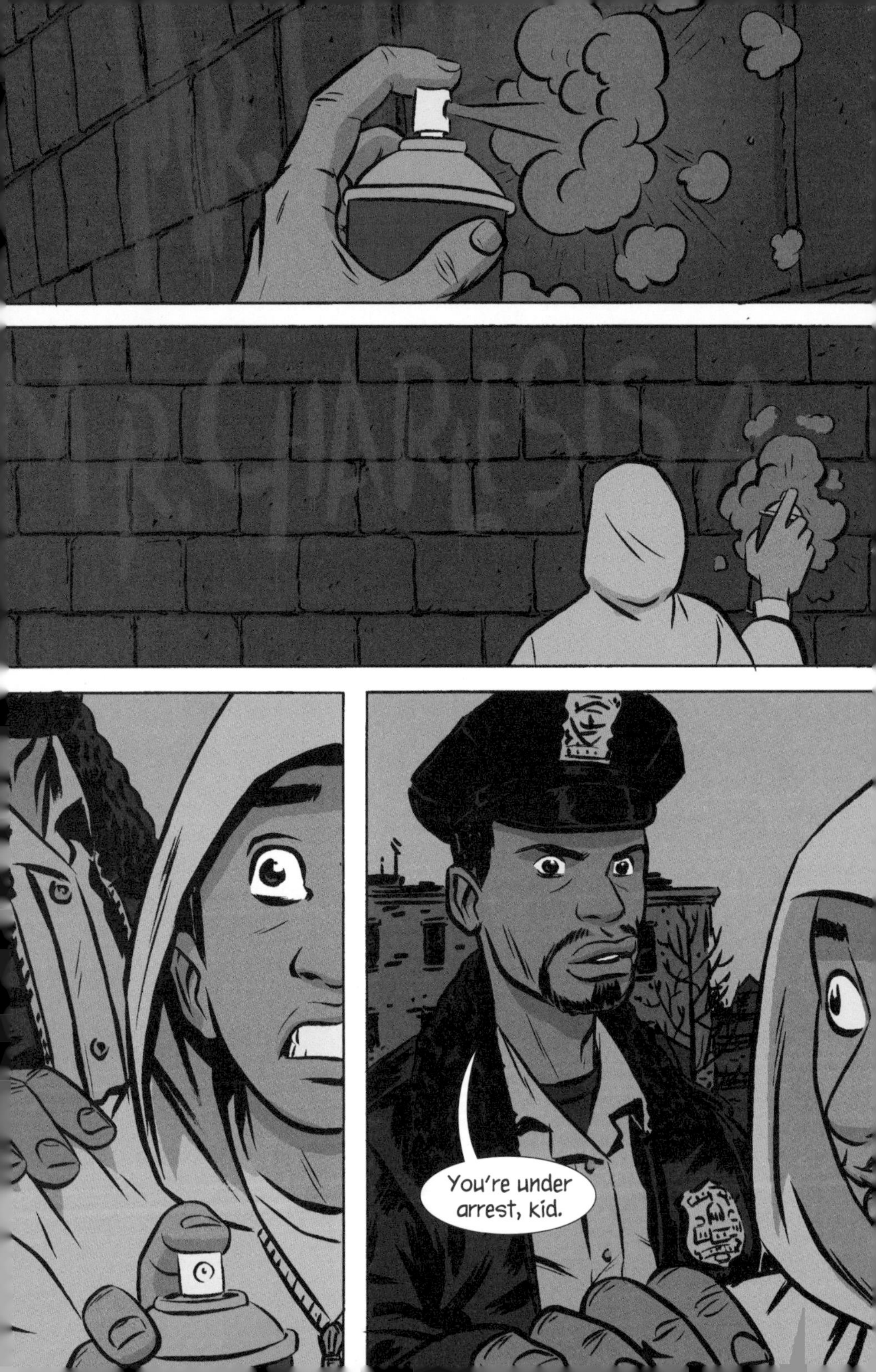
You're under arrest, kid.

CHAPTER 2
CUFFED

Anton could hardly breathe. His index finger still pressed down on the nozzle of the spray paint can. The blotch of red paint next to the "A" was getting bigger and paint was running down the wall.

"Why don't you drop the can, kid," the policeman said. "And put your hands on your head."

Anton tried to say "yes sir," but he couldn't speak. Instead, he nodded slowly. He felt his right hand open, and the can dropped to the cement with a loud clank.

Anton put both hands behind his head. He felt handcuffs slap onto his right wrist.

"Drop your hands behind your back," the policeman ordered next. Anton obeyed, and then felt the other cuff on his left wrist.

"Now turn around," the cop said. His voice was cold and deep. Anton shivered and turned around.

The cop was black, like Anton, and didn't even seem much older than Anton — maybe 22 years old. He was in full uniform, with a gun at his hip. Anton was glad to see it wasn't in the cop's hand.

"Come on," the policeman said. He led Anton down the sidewalk. A police car was around the corner. The officer opened the car door and held down Anton's head to help him in.

The door slammed as Anton slid across the seat. He watched the officer walk around the car, then climb into the driver's seat. *This is not good,* Anton thought.

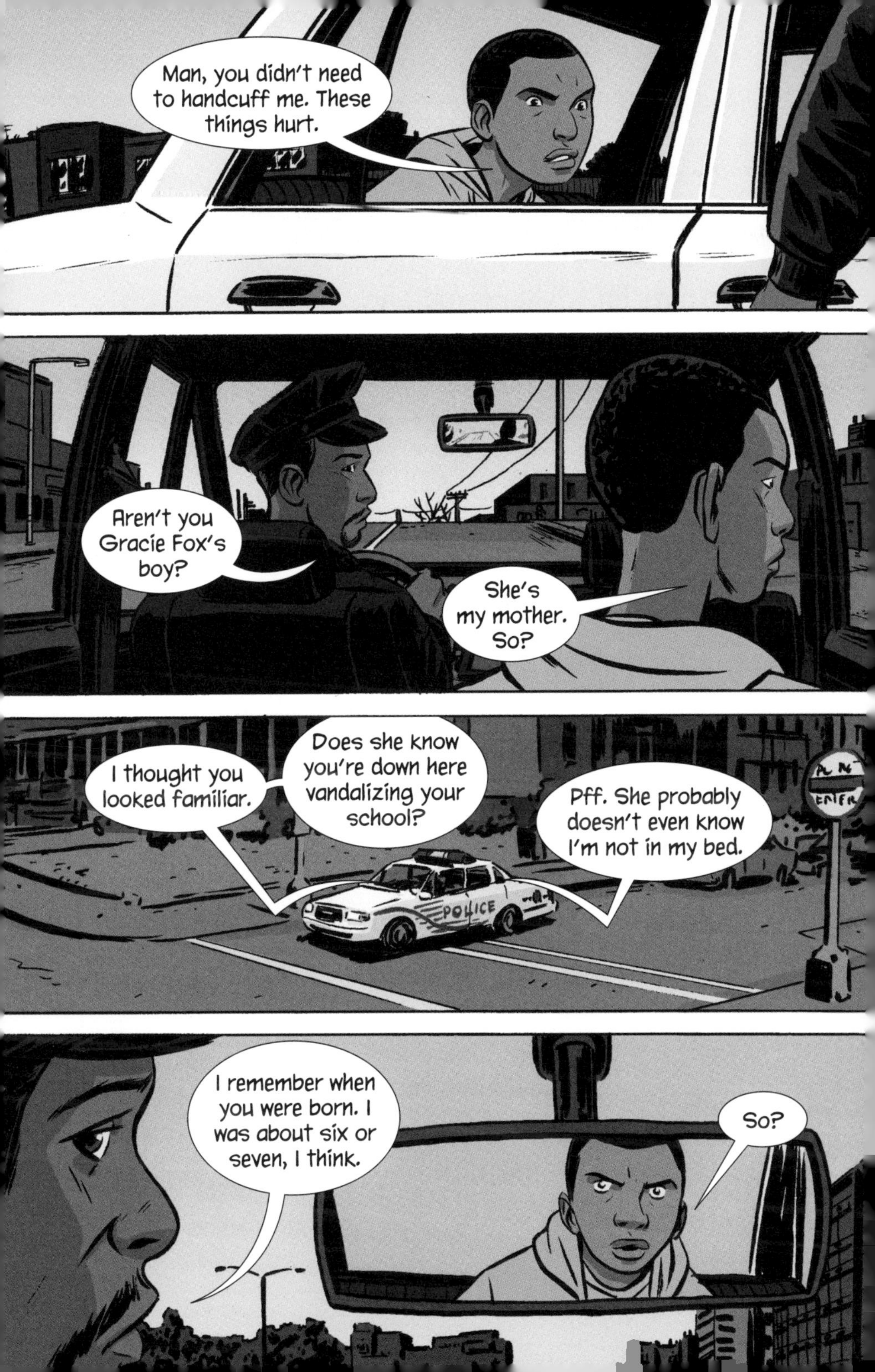
Man, you didn't need to handcuff me. These things hurt.
Aren't you Gracie Fox's boy?
She's my mother. So?
I thought you looked familiar.
Does she know you're down here vandalizing your school?
Pff. She probably doesn't even know I'm not in my bed.
POLICE
I remember when you were born. I was about six or seven, I think.
So?

The cop smiled. "So you're what now?" he asked. "About thirteen?"

"Fourteen," Anton said back.

As the car turned onto Martin Luther King Jr. Avenue, Anton spotted the police station up ahead. "This is stupid," Anton said. "I can't believe I'm going to jail for writing on the school."

The policeman pulled into the station parking lot. He got out of the car, then walked around and opened the door for Anton. "You know, I never liked Mr. Charles much either," the cop said. "He was tough."

"You went to that school too?" Anton asked.

"Of course," the officer replied. "I told you I remember your mom. We grew up in the same building."

"Dang," Anton said. "And now you're a cop?"

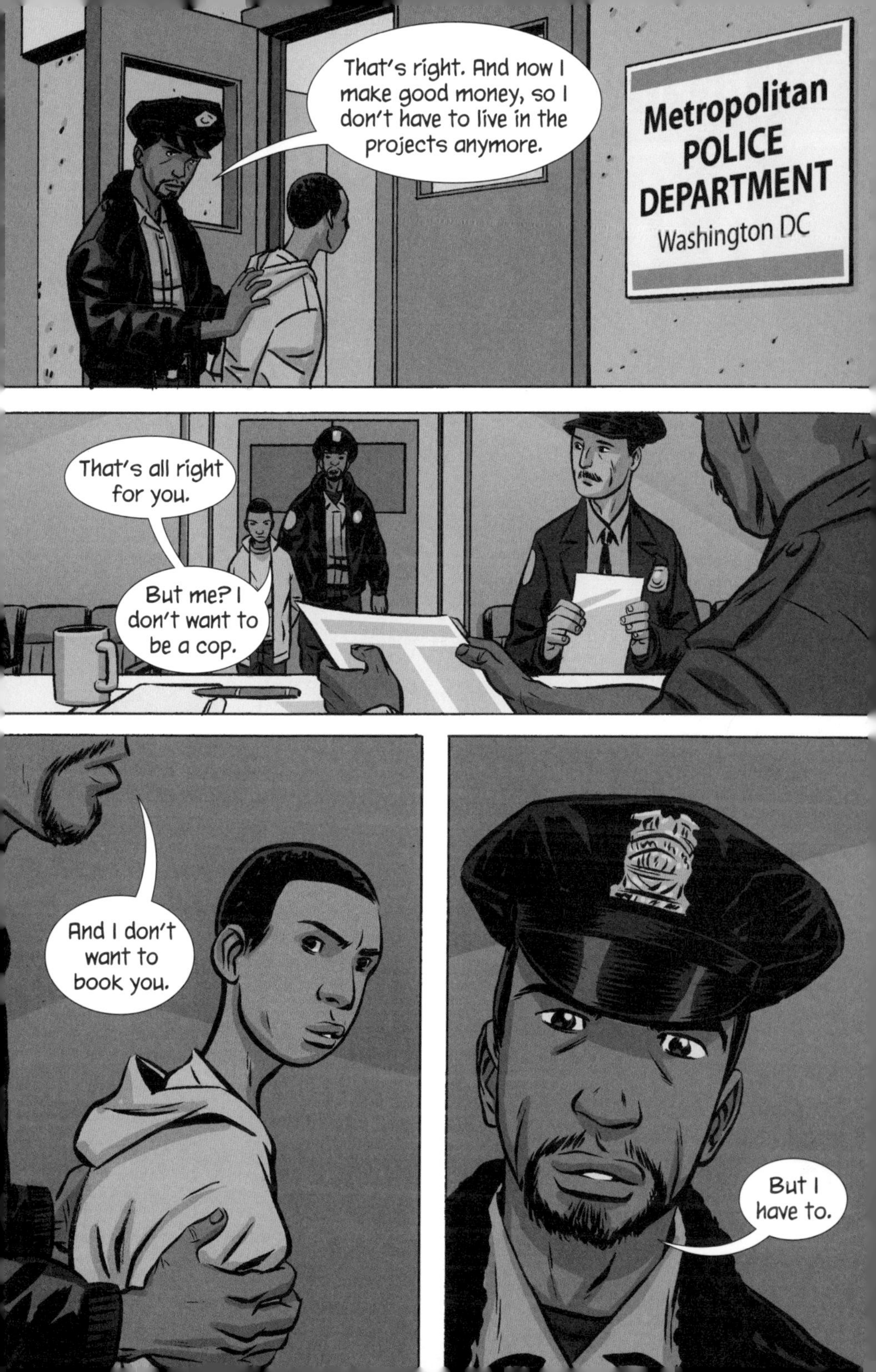

That's right. And now I make good money, so I don't have to live in the projects anymore.
Metropolitan POLICE DEPARTMENT Washington DC
That's all right for you.
But me? I don't want to be a cop.
And I don't want to book you.
But I have to.

CHAPTER 3

AT THE PRECINCT

"What do we have here, Griggs?" the old man at the desk asked.

The officer who had caught Anton fumbled with his keys a moment, then removed Anton's handcuffs. "This is one Anton Fox," Officer Griggs replied. "Being charged with misdemeanor property defacement."

Anton rolled his eyes. The old man at the desk didn't look at him, but entered something into a computer and then pulled out a slip of paper.

"Put your hand up here, Mr. Fox," the old man said.

"What for?" Anton asked.

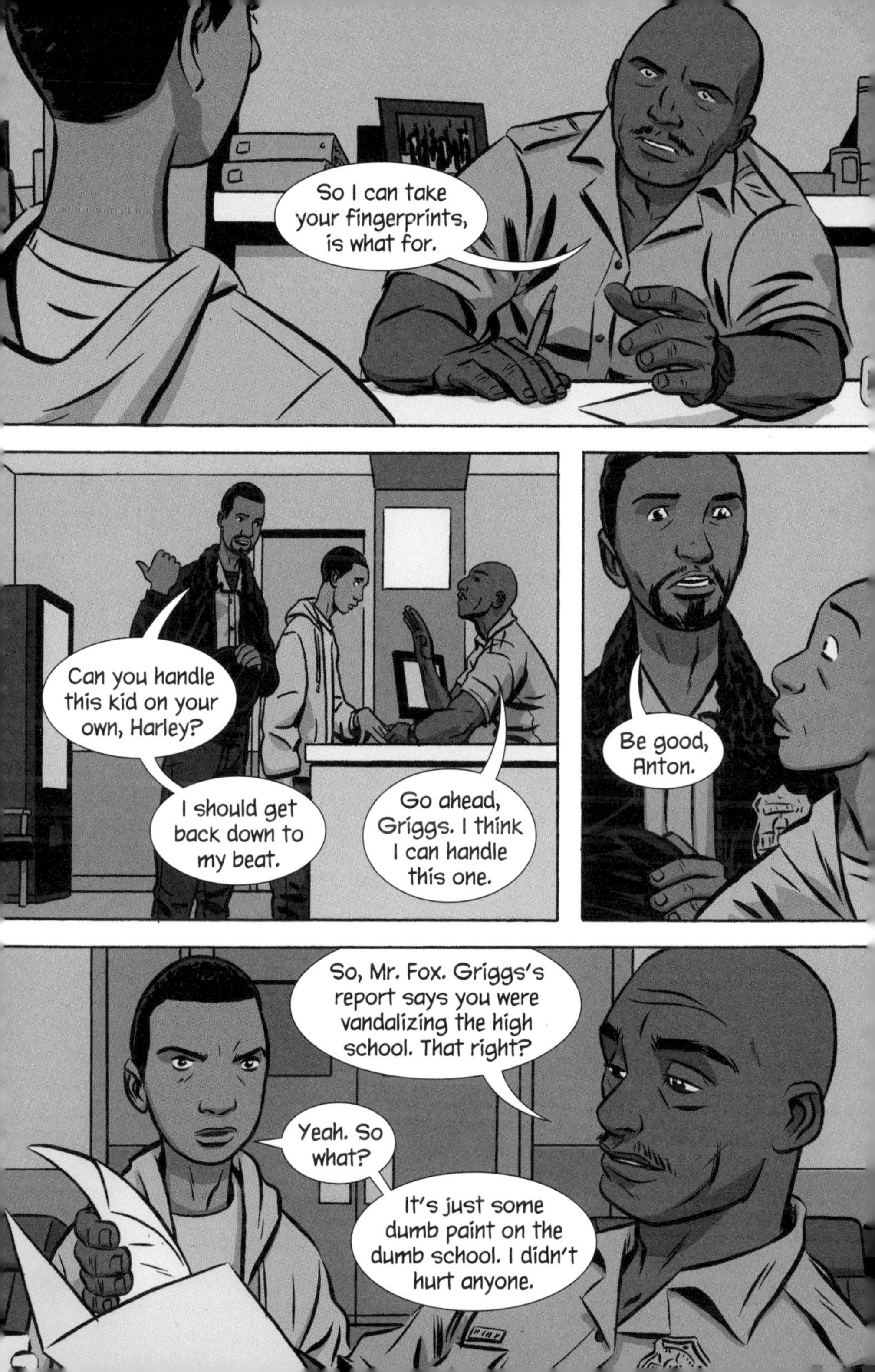
So I can take your fingerprints, is what for.
Can you handle this kid on your own, Harley?
I should get back down to my beat.
Go ahead, Griggs. I think I can handle this one.
Be good, Anton.
So, Mr. Fox. Griggs's report says you were vandalizing the high school. That right?
Yeah. So what?
It's just some dumb paint on the dumb school. I didn't hurt anyone.

Officer Harley shook his head. "You did, though," he said. "You hurt yourself."

Anton laughed. "Man, I'm fine," he said.

"Not if you keep up this attitude," Officer Harley said. He turned to the computer and hit a few keys. "Because if you make yourself a regular down here at the precinct, you'll have one sad life."

Anton waved him off. "Come on," he said. "Like a kid like me — a kid from the Congress Housing Projects — is going to make it anyway."

"Isn't Officer Griggs from the Congress Housing Projects?" Harley replied. He smirked.

"Man, like I told him," Anton said. "I don't want to be a cop. So what good is that for me?"

Officer Harley sighed. "No one's telling you to become a cop," he said. "Though you could do worse, believe me."

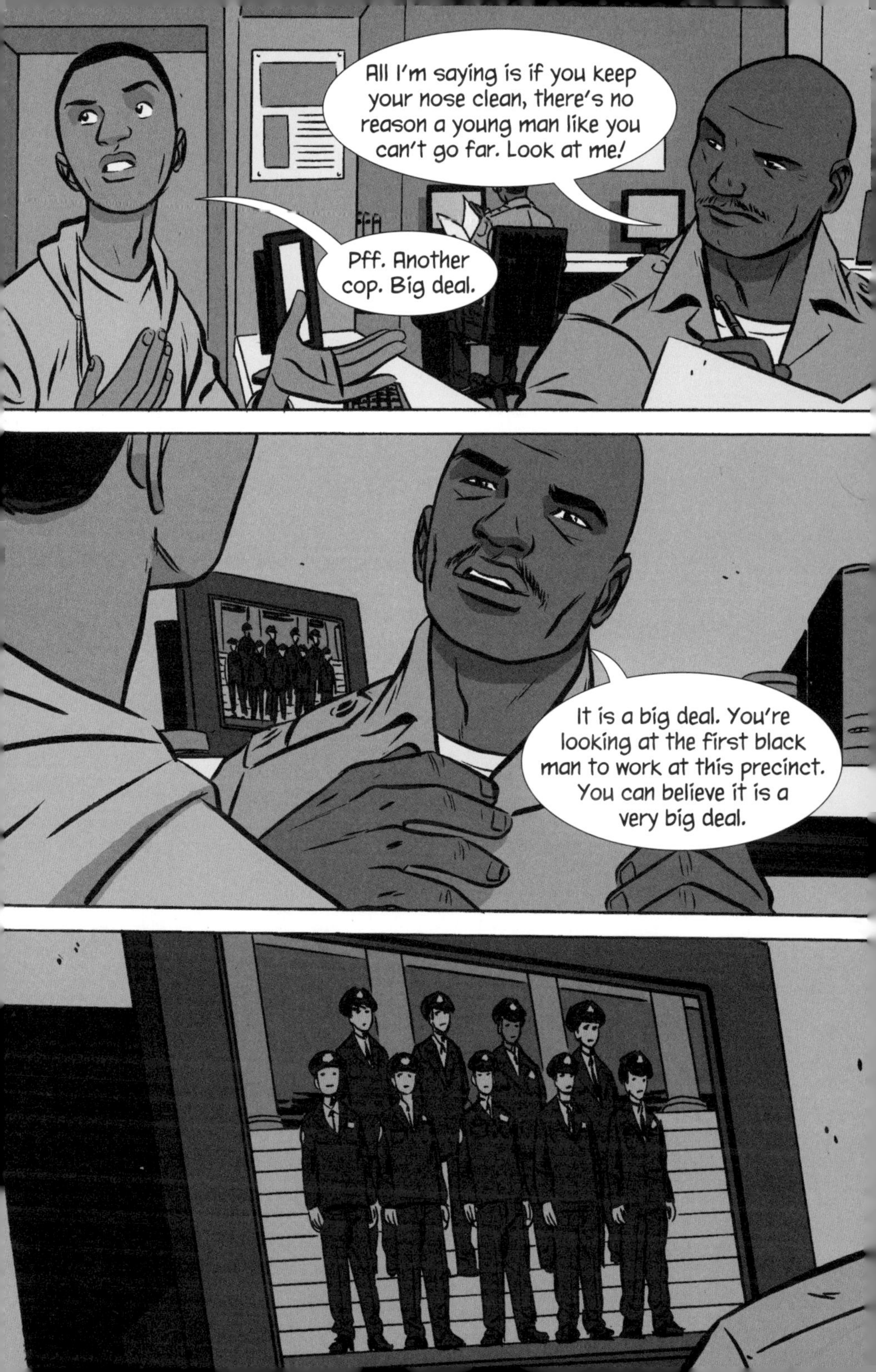
All I'm saying is if you keep your nose clean, there's no reason a young man like you can't go far. Look at me!
Pff. Another cop. Big deal.
It is a big deal. You're looking at the first black man to work at this precinct. You can believe it is a very big deal.

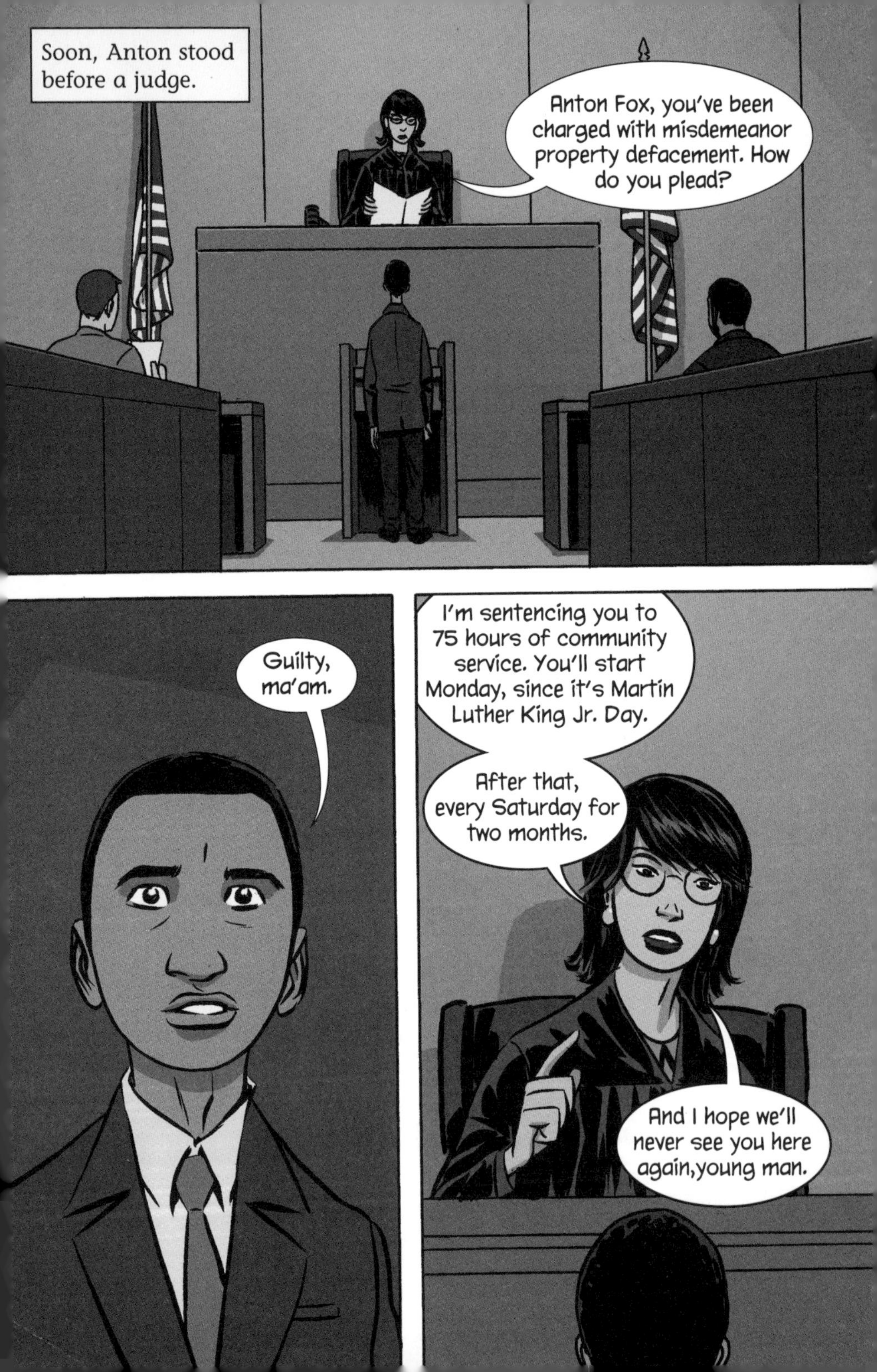
Soon, Anton stood before a judge.
Anton Fox, you've been charged with misdemeanor property defacement. How do you plead?
Guilty, ma'am.
I'm sentencing you to 75 hours of community service. You'll start Monday, since it's Martin Luther King Jr. Day.
After that, every Saturday for two months.
And I hope we'll never see you here again,young man.

CHAPTER 4

BACK HOME

"Mom, I get it, okay?" Anton said as he walked into their apartment at the Congress Housing Project. "You don't have to keep repeating it."

"Don't I?" his mother said. She slammed the apartment door behind her. "Because I don't think I can possibly say it enough. I can't believe I just had to go down to the precinct and get my son out of a holding cell!"

"It's not a big deal," Anton said. "Besides, if one of us should be mad, it's me."

"You?!" Anton's mom said. She looked like she was about to blow up with anger. "Why should you be mad, exactly?"

"Because I got busted," Anton explained, "and I'll have to go out working all day Monday because of it. Not to mention the next two months of Saturdays!"

His mother pulled off her coat and hung it in the front closet. "That's the best part of all of this," she said. "You'll be kept out of trouble for at least one day per week."

"Oh, come on, Mom," Anton said. He slumped down onto the couch.

"Plus, it's good for everyone to have you clean up the National Mall before the inauguration on Tuesday," Mom added. "The eyes of the world will be on the Mall that day."

"Yeah," Anton said, his voice thick with sarcasm, "it's a huge deal."

"It is a huge deal," Mom snapped.

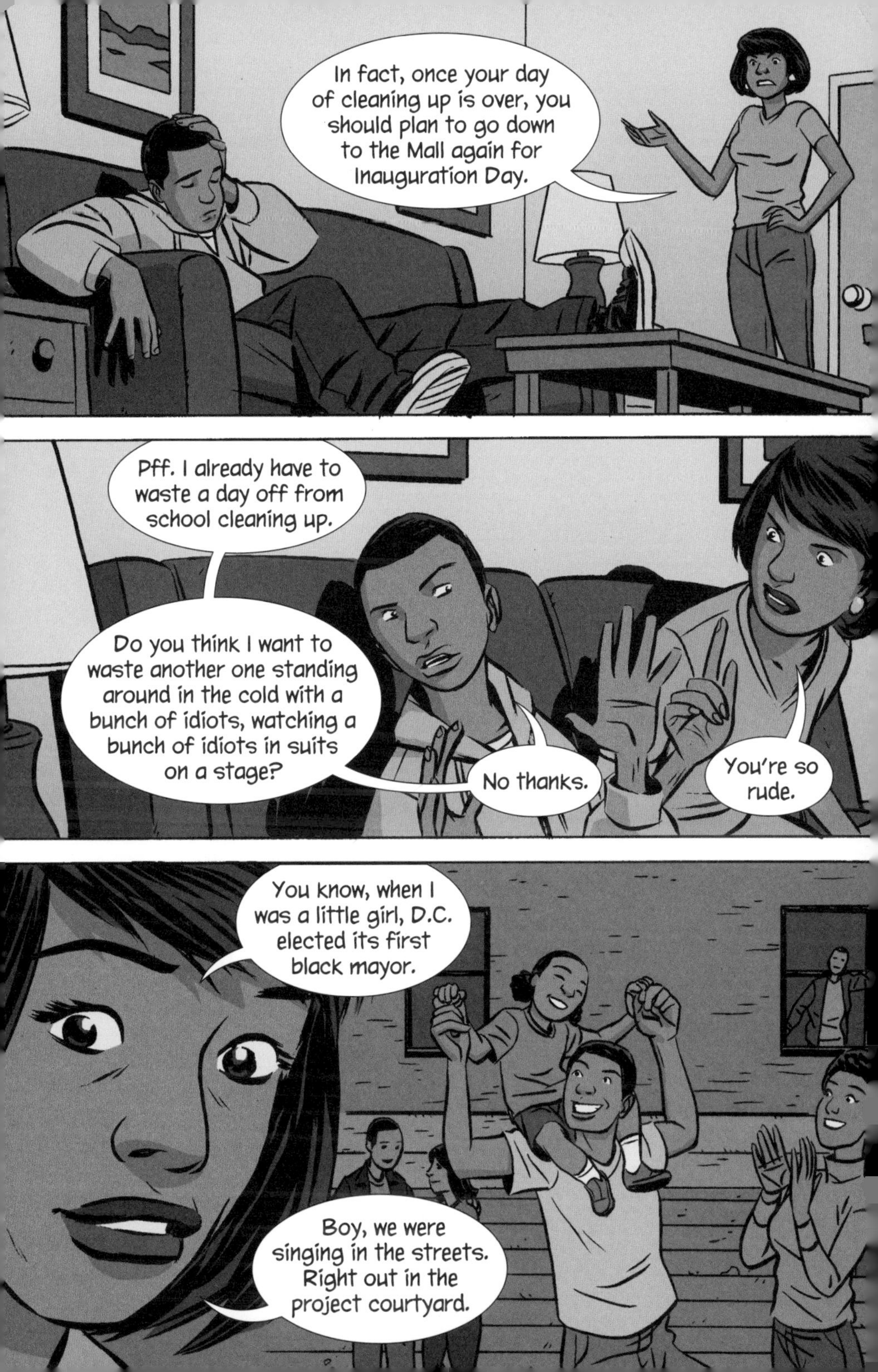
In fact, once your day of cleaning up is over, you should plan to go down to the Mall again for Inauguration Day.
Pff. I already have to waste a day off from school cleaning up.
Do you think I want to waste another one standing around in the cold with a bunch of idiots, watching a bunch of idiots in suits on a stage?
No thanks.
You're so rude.
You know, when I was a little girl, D.C. elected its first black mayor.
Boy, we were singing in the streets. Right out in the project courtyard.

"So?" Anton said.

"So you're lucky to be alive today, Anton," Mom replied, "when a young man from these projects really does have a good chance to make something of himself."

"Right," Anton said. He flipped through the channels quickly. "I'm the next president, right? Maybe a future billionaire."

"It could be, son," Mom said. "But only if you keep that head on straight and stop fooling around with graffiti, and failing math classes. You know what I mean?"

Anton shrugged.

His mother put a hand on his chin, turning him to face her. "Do you know what I mean?"

"Yes, okay?" Anton said. "I know what you mean."

CHAPTER 5
CLEANING UP

"Why do they have to start this so early?" Anton whined. It was Monday morning, and he and his mom were on the bus heading toward the National Mall.

"This is a punishment, Anton," Mom replied, "not a vacation. You better not start whining once you get down there, either. You did the crime, and now you're going to pay for it. And I hope that is clear. Is it?"

"Yeah, it's clear," Anton said. "It's just early, that's all."

Anton watched out the window as the bus crossed the Anacostia River and headed into the heart of Washington, D.C.

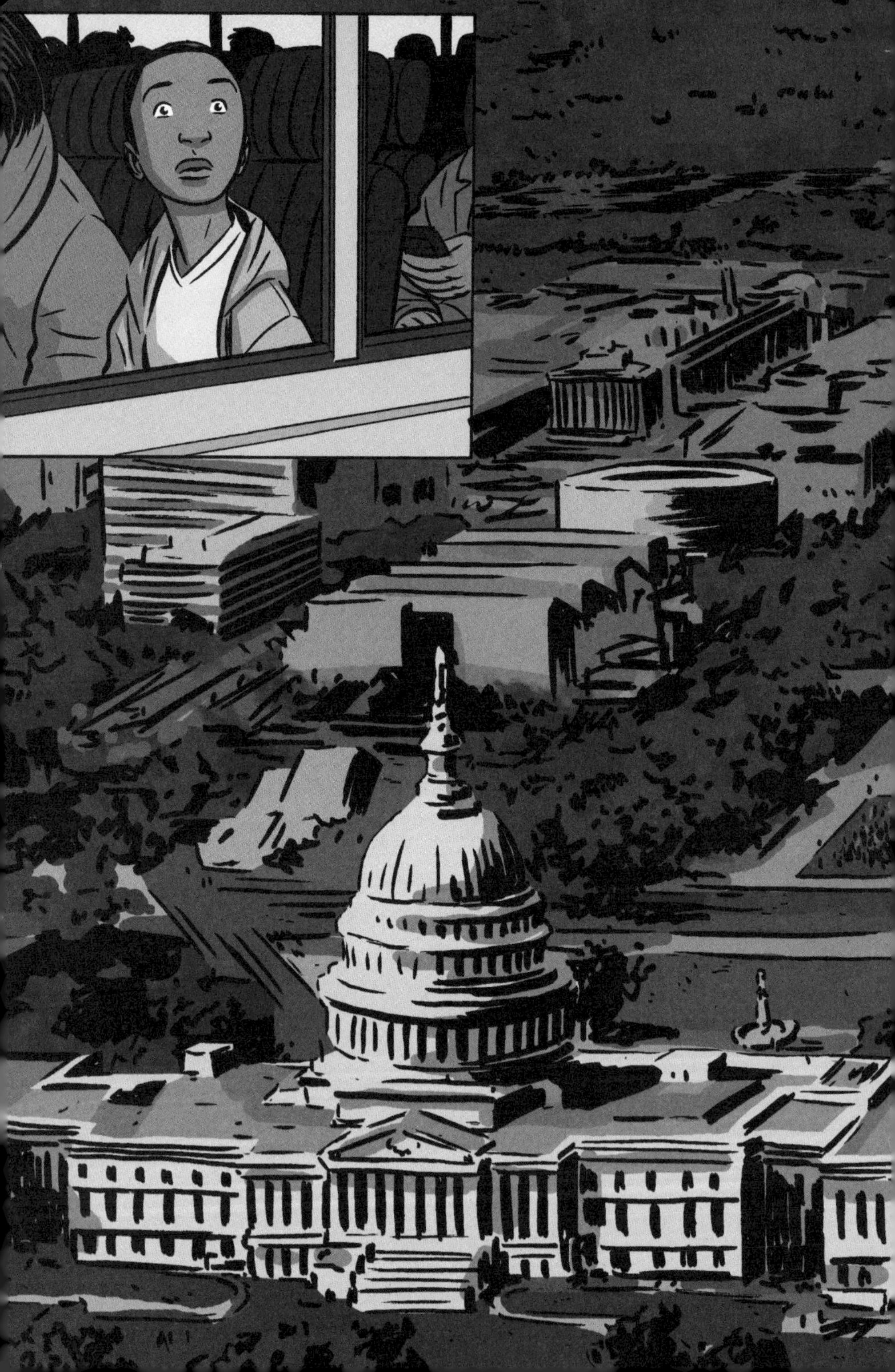

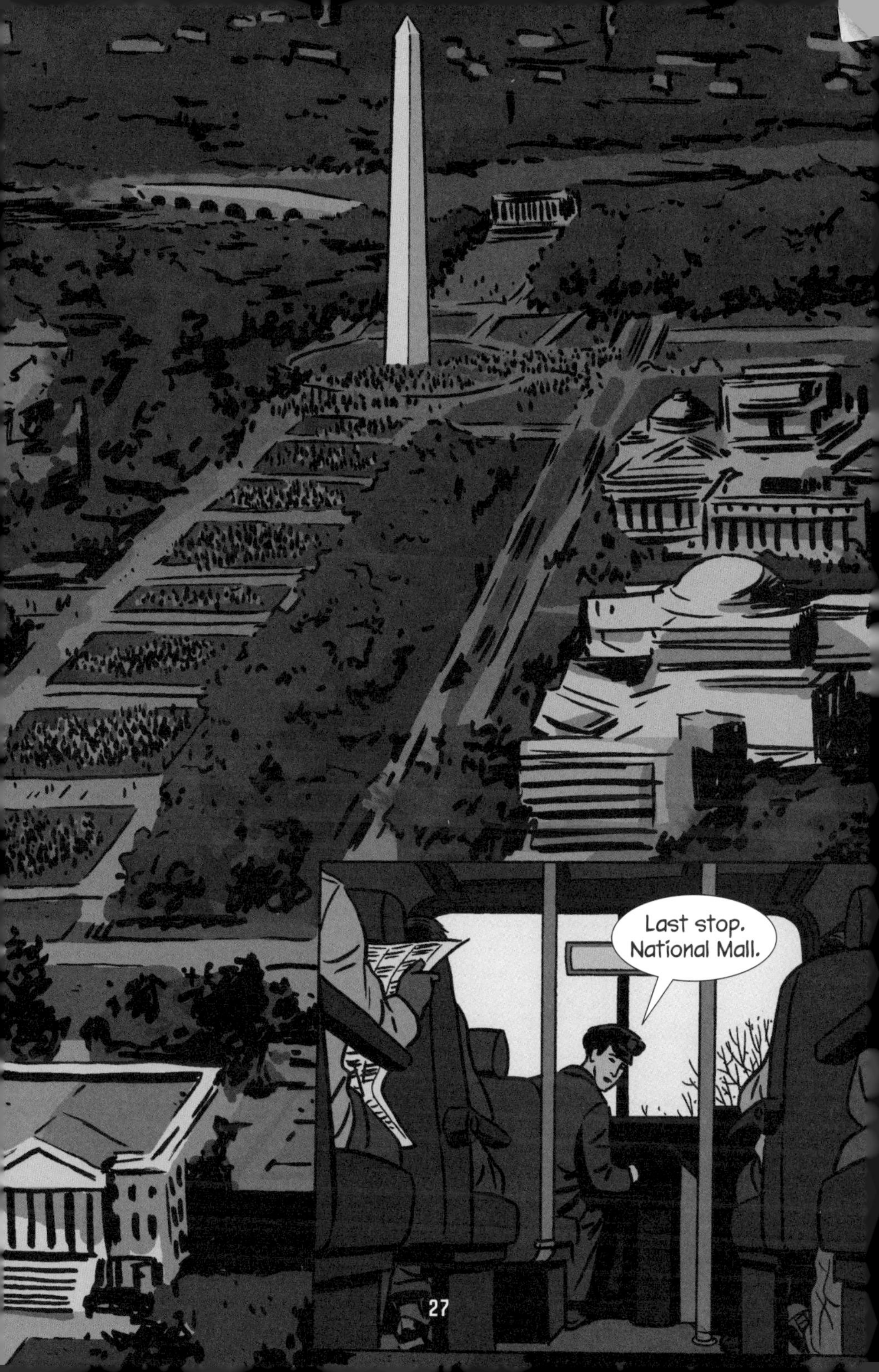
Last stop. National Mall.

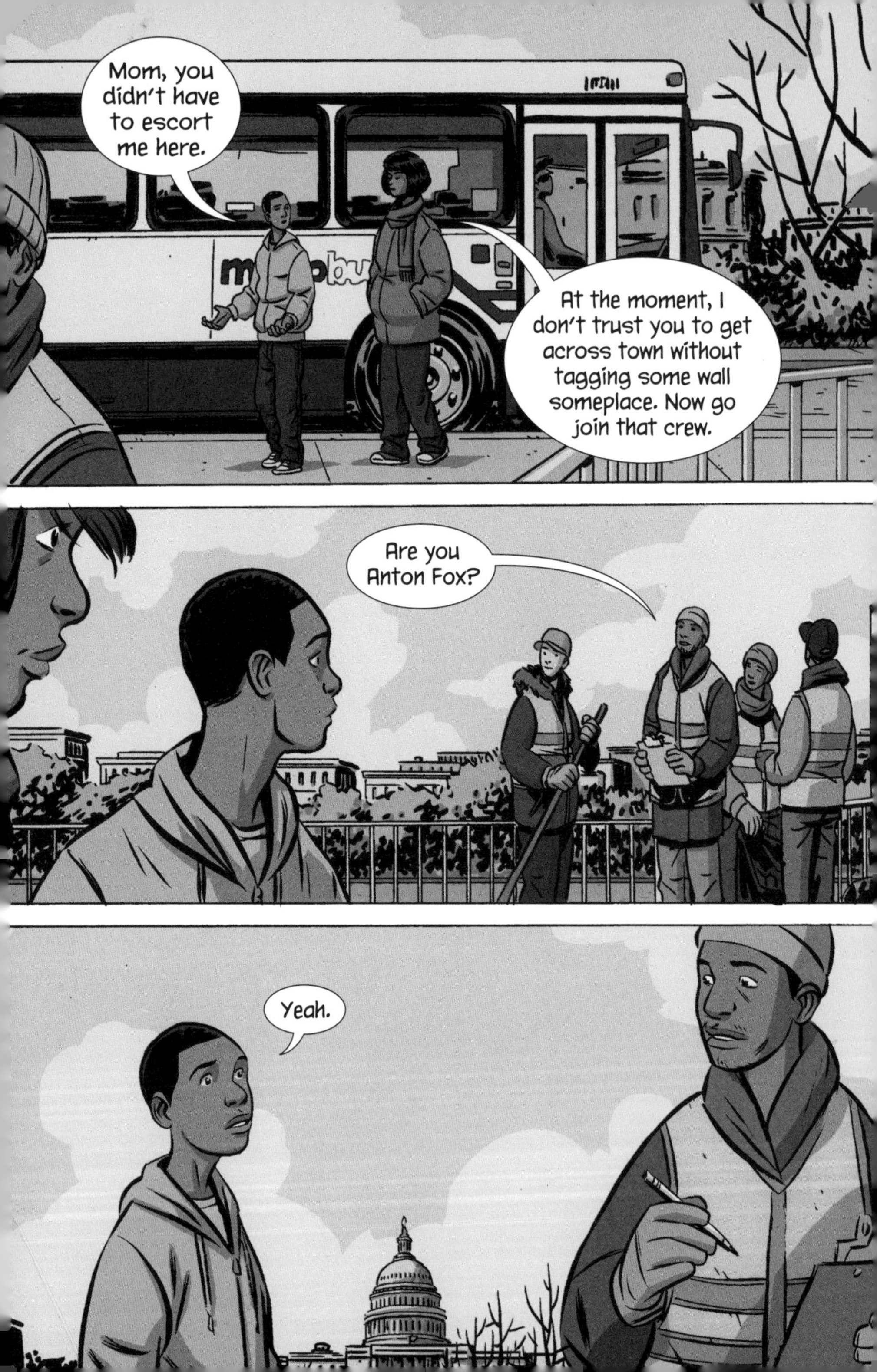
Mom, you didn't have to escort me here.
At the moment, I don't trust you to get across town without tagging some wall someplace. Now go join that crew.
Are you Anton Fox?
Yeah.

"Put this on," the man said, and he tossed him an orange vest like the others were wearing. "I'm Paolo. I'm a volunteer here, and I'm in charge of the cleanup crew the city sent us this morning."

"Okay," Anton said. He slipped the vest on over his down jacket.

"And that crew includes you," Paolo went on. "And that makes twenty of us. So we can get started."

Paolo went on to explain what kind of cleaning they'd be doing, and what section of the Mall each cleaner was responsible for. After his speech, the crew dispersed to start their work.

Anton was given a big section on the south end of the Mall. He began picking up cans and torn newspapers and empty bottles, and putting them in the thick black plastic bag Paolo had given him.

It wasn't long before the bag was full. Anton looked around, wondering what to do with his full bag, and where to get another bag to use.

"Can I help you with something, Mr. Fox?" Paolo said. He headed over to Anton.

"Yeah, my bag is full," Anton said. "Does that mean I'm done for the day?"

Paolo laughed and looked at his watch. "No, you've still got about seven and a half hours to go," he said.

He pulled out an empty bag and gave it to Anton. "Tie off that full one and drop it in the corner of your zone," Paolo said. "We'll collect all the full bags at the end of the day."

Anton shook his head. "Man, this is going to be a long day," he said.

Paolo nodded. "It's an important day, too," he said.

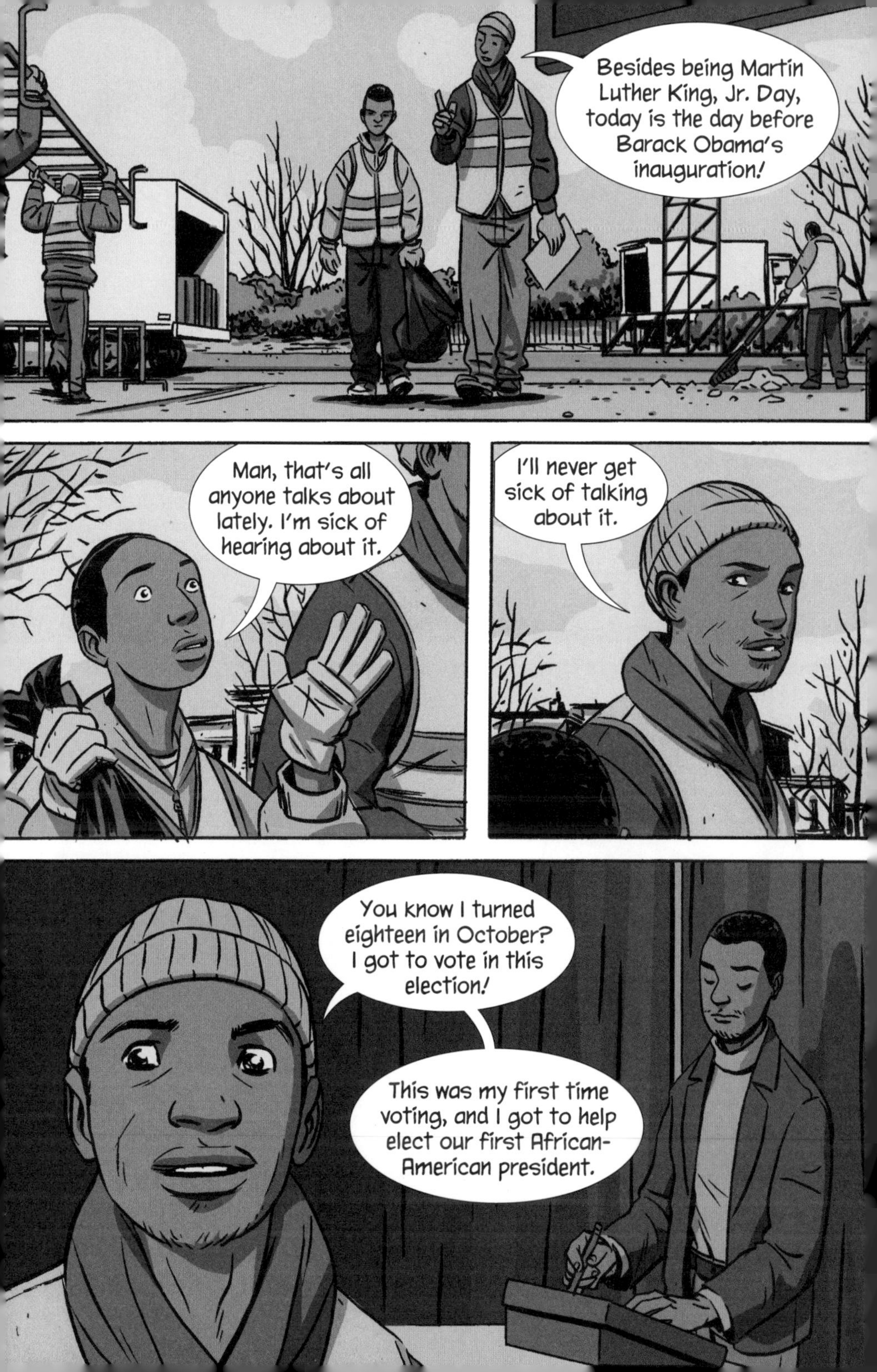
Besides being Martin Luther King, Jr. Day, today is the day before Barack Obama's inauguration!
Man, that's all anyone talks about lately. I'm sick of hearing about it.
I'll never get sick of talking about it.
You know I turned eighteen in October? I got to vote in this election!
This was my first time voting, and I got to help elect our first African-American president.

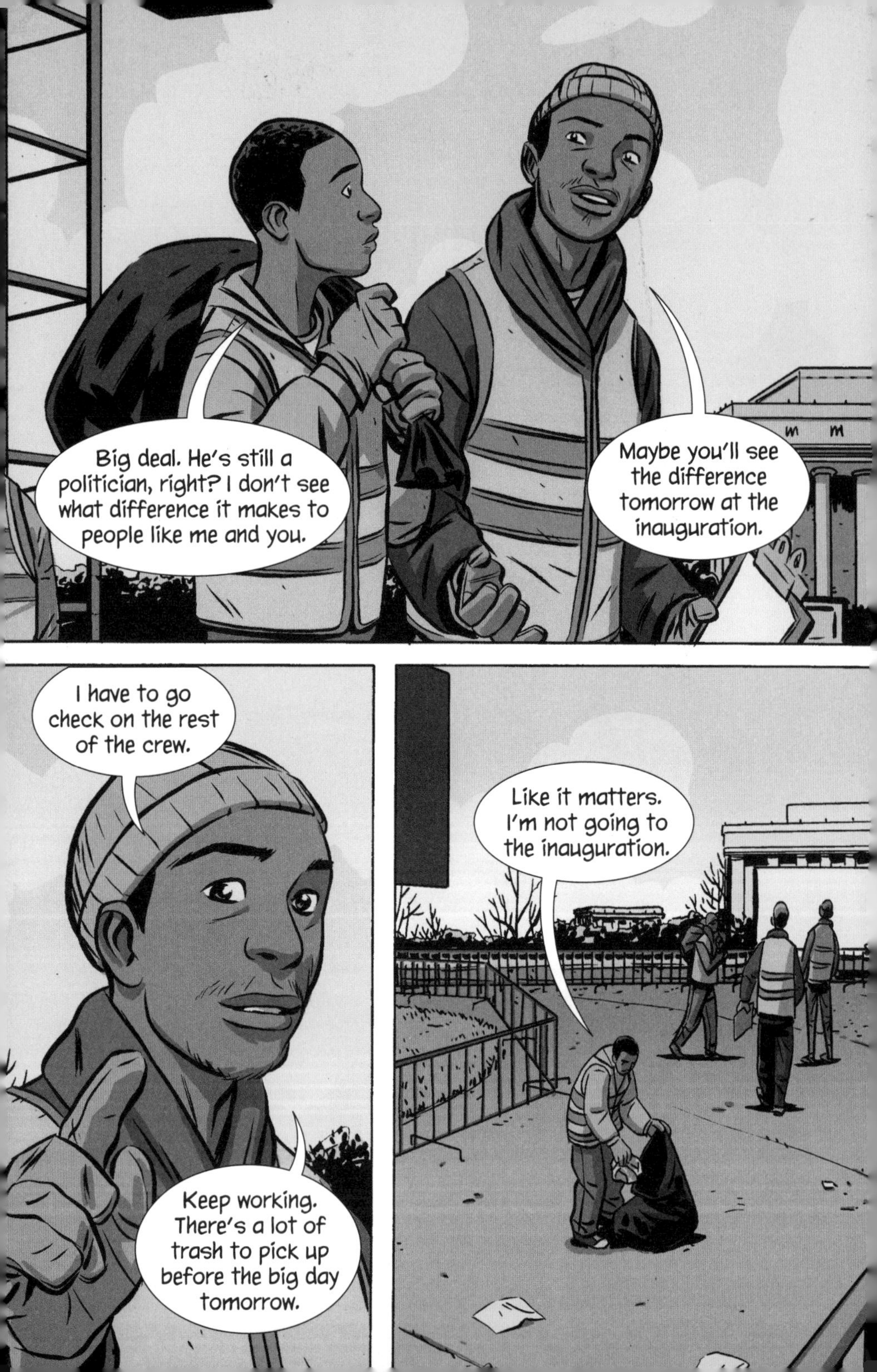
Big deal. He's still a politician, right? I don't see what difference it makes to people like me and you.
Maybe you'll see the difference tomorrow at the inauguration.
I have to go check on the rest of the crew.
Keep working. There's a lot of trash to pick up before the big day tomorrow.
Like it matters. I'm not going to the inauguration.

CHAPTER 6
MOM'S PUNISHMENT

Anton dragged his tired body up the stairs of his building. The sun was long down, and on the bus ride home, he'd fallen asleep. Anton had never worked so hard in one day in all his life.

Anton pulled off his gloves and found his apartment key in his coat pocket. With his hand shaking, it was tough to get the key into the door. But finally he pushed the door open and fell inside.

"I'm home," he called out.

His mom came out of the kitchen. "Hey, they worked you pretty hard, huh?" she asked.

Anton collapsed onto the couch without pulling off his coat.

His mother chuckled. "Well, you had it coming, I suppose," she said.

Anton gaped at her. "I can't believe I have to do this again for the next ten weekends!" he said.

"You got off easy!" his mom said. "Disrespecting Mr. Charles and your school — and the whole community — like that!"

Anton nodded. "I know, I know," he said. "Can I go to sleep now please?" He stretched out on the couch and closed his eyes. He could feel himself falling asleep.

His mom laughed. "Sure, sleep," she said. "You need your rest, because tomorrow morning, bright and early, you and I are heading back to the Mall."

"What?!" Anton said as his eyes shot open. "Mom, I don't have to go back until next weekend. Until then, I'm sleeping."

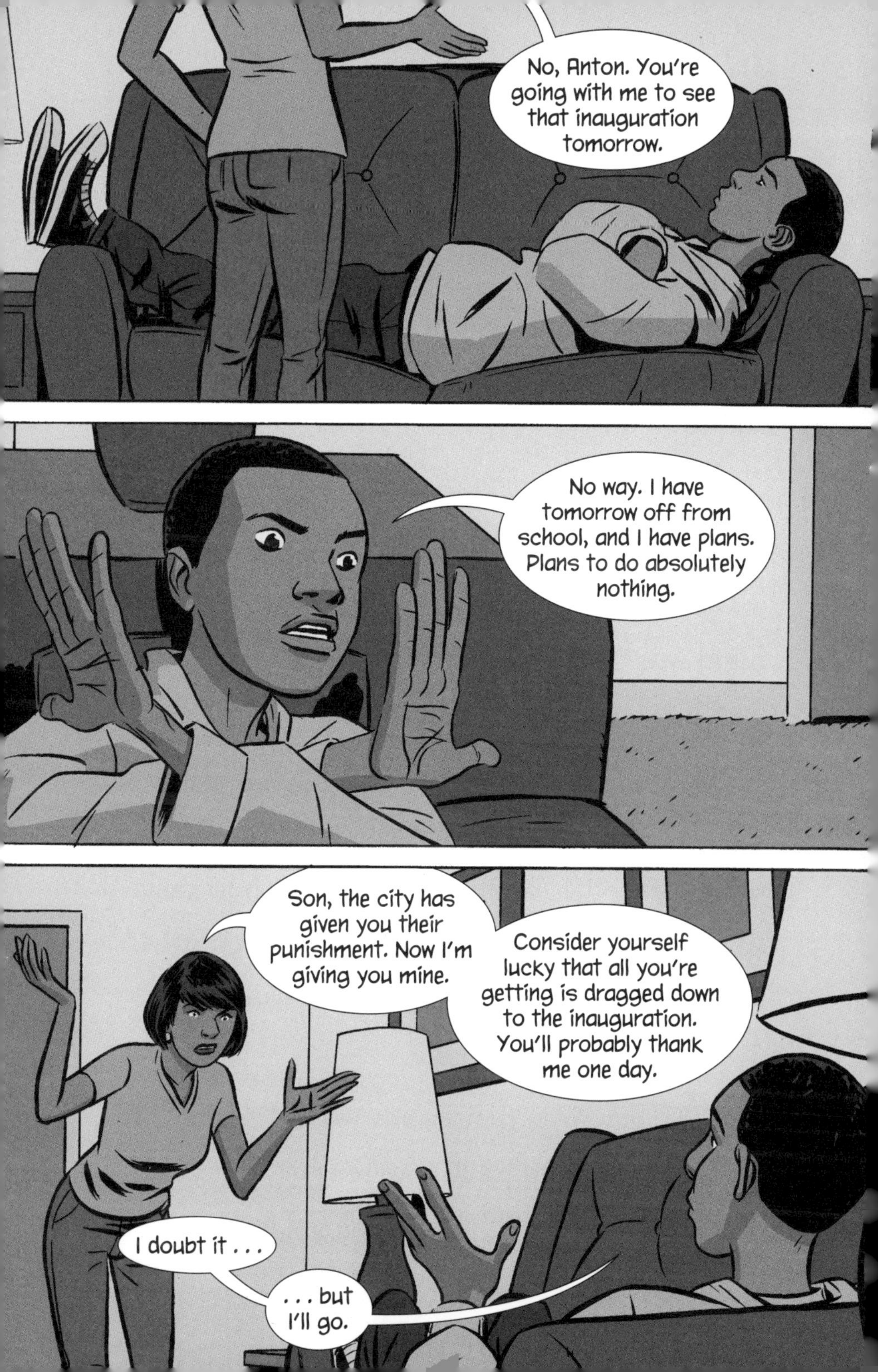
No, Anton. You're going with me to see that inauguration tomorrow.
No way. I have tomorrow off from school, and I have plans. Plans to do absolutely nothing.
Son, the city has given you their punishment. Now I'm giving you mine.
Consider yourself lucky that all you're getting is dragged down to the inauguration. You'll probably thank me one day.
I doubt it . . .
. . . but I'll go.

CHAPTER 7

THE MARCH

Anton wasn't sure if he was really awake. It was so early, the sun hadn't even started to come up yet. The moon was still up, and the cold, clear night was filled with as many stars as one could ever hope to see inside the city sky.

Anton stood with his mom at the bus stop outside Congress Housing Project, along with about fifty other people. He didn't see how they would all fit on the next bus. Sure enough, when it came along it was full already. It didn't even stop.

His mom, even though she was shivering with cold, laughed. "Looks like we're walking!" she shouted, almost with glee, it seemed to Anton.

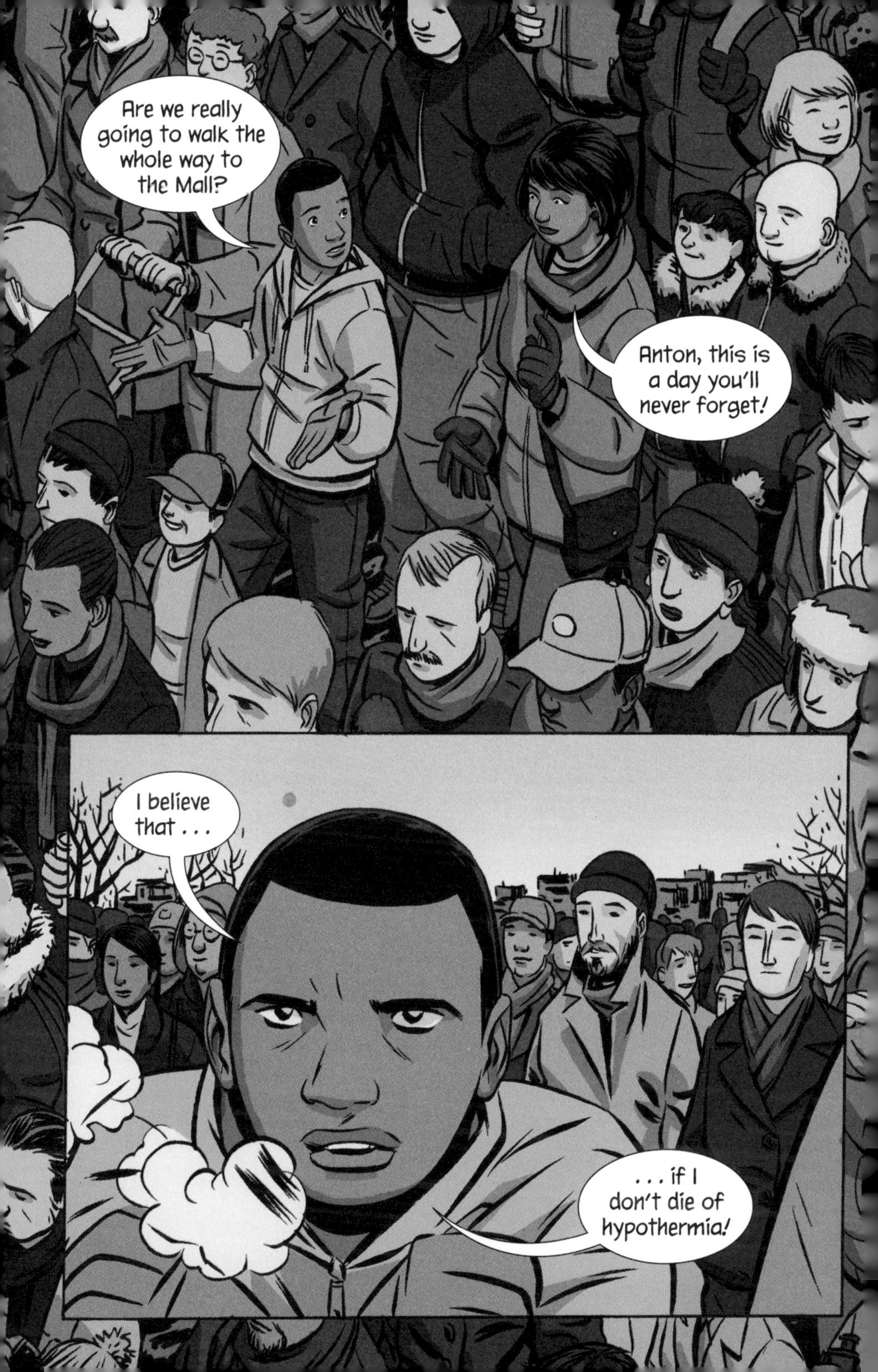
Are we really going to walk the whole way to the Mall?
Anton, this is a day you'll never forget!
I believe that . . .
. . . if I don't die of hypothermia!

"I can't believe this many people are up this early," Anton shouted to his mother.

"And I," Mom replied, "can't believe anyone could be sleeping!"

The cold wind on the river was bone chilling. The group huddled together against the gusts and marched on. By the time they reached the north side of the river, it seemed to Anton, there must have been well over a thousand of them.

As they strode along Pennsylvania Avenue, with the White House all lit up and sun just beginning to peek above the horizon to the east, more people joined them.

There were people from other parts of the city, coming together to march to the National Mall. Anton imagined similar groups forming north of the Mall, and west of it, representing all the neighborhoods of the capital.

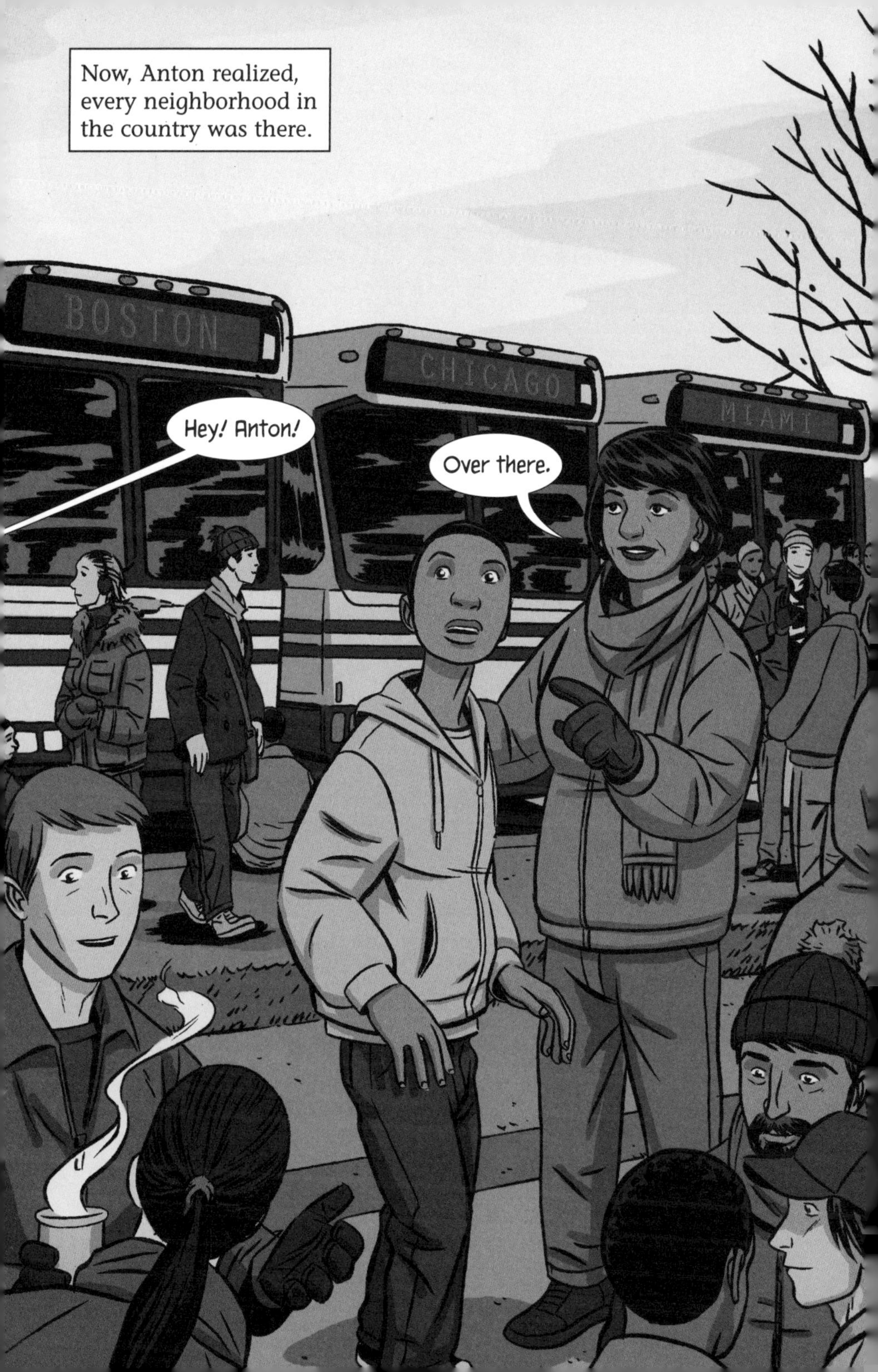
Now, Anton realized, every neighborhood in the country was there.
BOSTON
CHICAGO
MIAMI
Hey! Anton!
Over there.

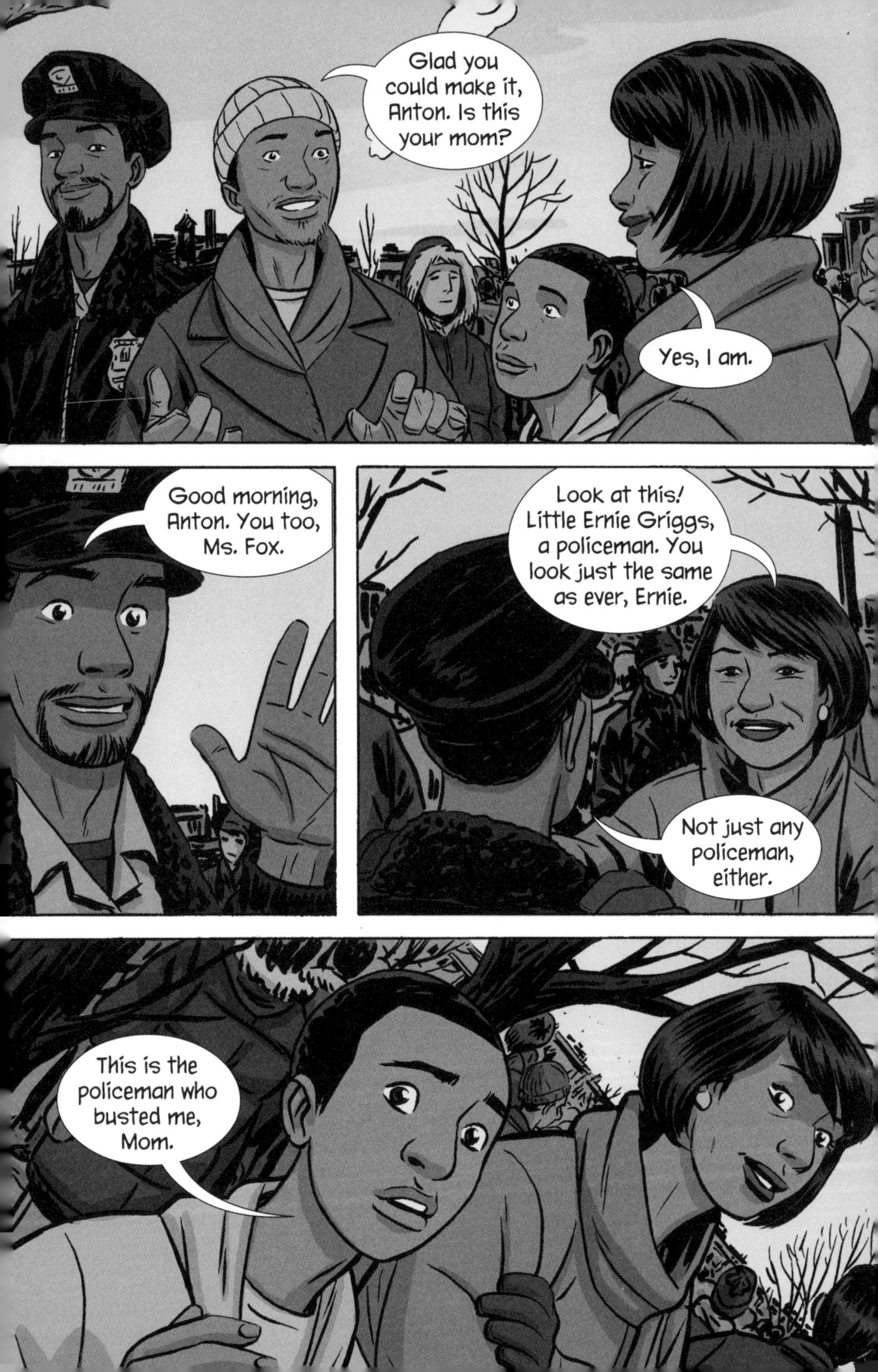
Glad you could make it, Anton. Is this your mom?
Yes, I am.
Good morning, Anton. You too, Ms. Fox.
Look at this! Little Ernie Griggs, a policeman. You look just the same as ever, Ernie.
Not just any policeman, either.
This is the policeman who busted me, Mom.

"He did the right thing, Anton," his mom said. "Ernie, I haven't seen you in years. Where have you been hiding?"

"I moved out of my parents' apartment at Congress, Ms. Fox," the officer replied. "I've got a house in Anacostia."

"You call me Gracie, okay?" she said. Then she turned to Anton. "You see that, Anton? I want you to stay straight so you can get out of Congress, own a home someday, not like me or your father ever did, rest his soul."

"Yeah, I see that, Mom," Anton replied.

Surrounded by Americans of every race, shape, color, and creed, Anton was finally starting to understand, too.

CHAPTER 8

PRESIDENT OBAMA

Officer Griggs led Anton, his mother, and Paolo toward the Mall. With a police escort, they were able to push themselves closer and closer to the roped-off VIP section. It was almost 10 a.m. by the time they stopped.

"When does Obama get sworn in?" Anton asked.

Paolo shrugged. Ms. Fox said, "Not soon enough."

Officer Griggs laughed. "Not for a couple more hours," he said.

It was the longest two hours of Anton's life, he felt. Besides the intense cold, the crowds were overwhelming, and so was the suspense.

The funny thing, he realized, was that in a way he'd been waiting for a moment like this for fourteen years. His mother had been waiting for more than twice that long. Officer Harley back at the precinct had been waiting for who knew how long.

But it never seemed like waiting before, not to Anton. Now that he really knew it was coming, soon but not quite yet, it was driving him crazy.

Finally, it was time. The ceremonies began with a string quartet performance, a poem, and a prayer. Aretha Franklin sang a song, which made Anton's mom cry.

Finally, the sun reached its highest point, though the day didn't seem to be getting any warmer. Then the president-elect took the stage.

Anton only knew this because the crowd ahead of him began to scream and shout: "Obama! Obama! Obama!"

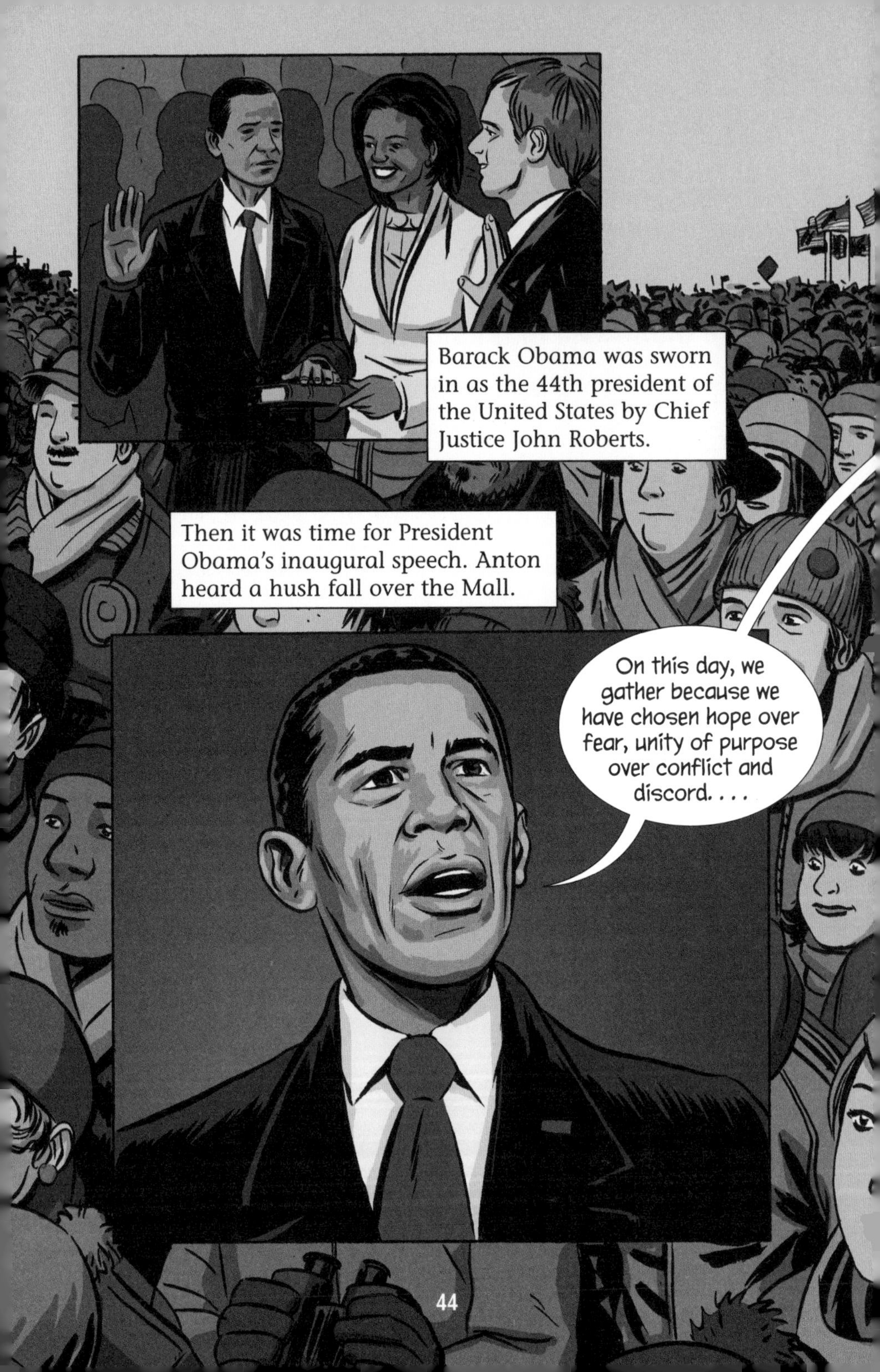
Barack Obama was sworn in as the 44th president of the United States by Chief Justice John Roberts.
Then it was time for President Obama's inaugural speech. Anton heard a hush fall over the Mall.
On this day, we gather because we have chosen hope over fear, unity of purpose over conflict and discord. . . .

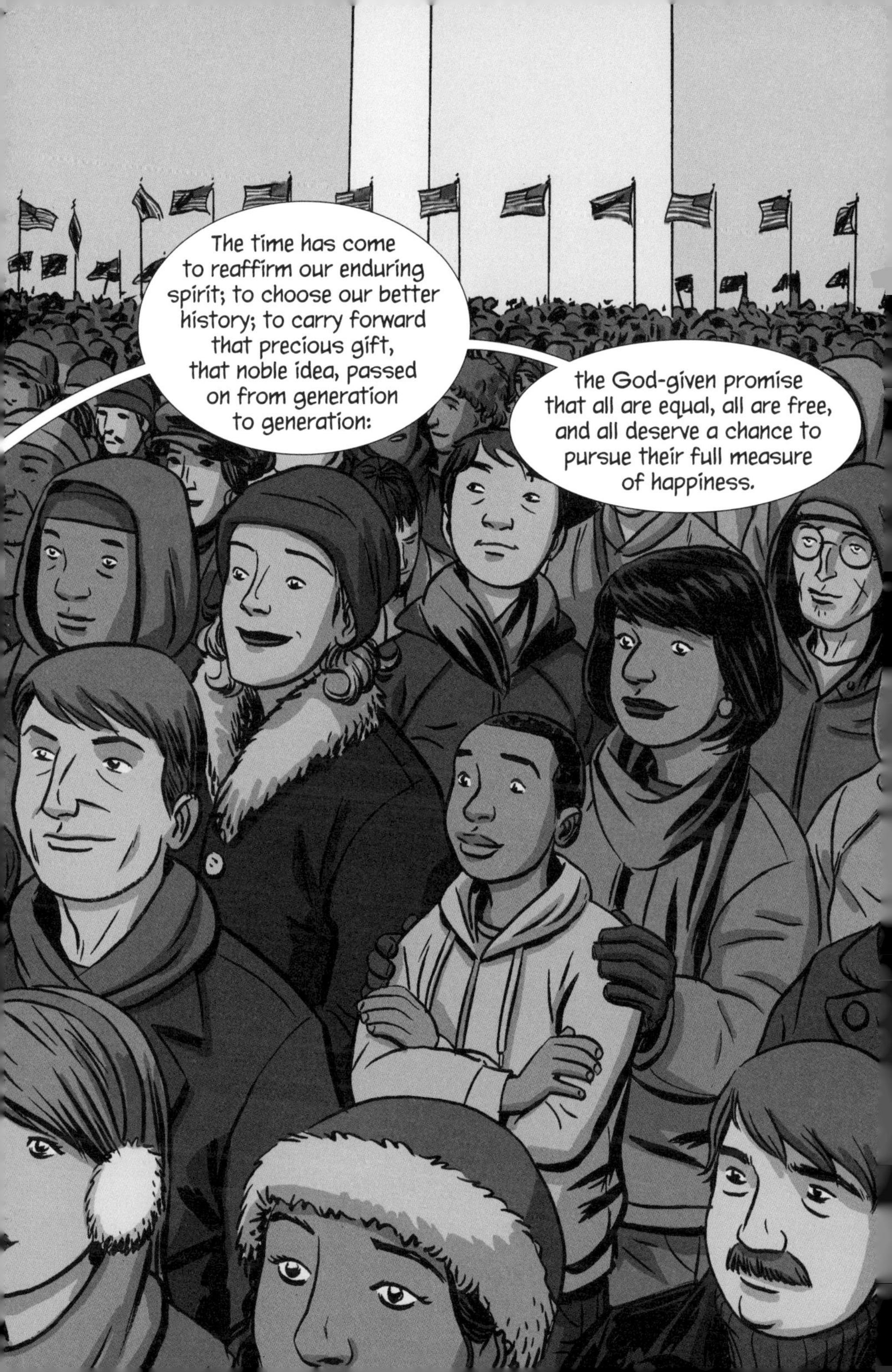
The time has come to reaffirm our enduring spirit; to choose our better history; to carry forward that precious gift, that noble idea, passed on from generation to generation:
the God-given promise that all are equal, all are free, and all deserve a chance to pursue their full measure of happiness.

"This is the meaning of our liberty and our creed, why men and women and children of every race and every faith can join in celebration across this magnificent mall," President Obama said. "And why a man whose father less than 60 years ago might not have been served at a local restaurant can now stand before you to take a most sacred oath."

A chill ran up Anton's spine, because it was true. If the new president's very own father had entered a luncheonette right there in that city, less than sixty years before — back when Anton's own grandparents were still living nearby — he would have been asked to leave, or put under arrest if he didn't. Segregation was two generations past, and now hope was a real thing.

Anton couldn't stop smiling.

CHAPTER 9
CHANGE HAS COME

The president's speech ended to huge applause. It roared over the mall and all over the center of Washington, DC.

Anton could swear he heard it ringing from every city in the nation, even from as far away as Kenya, Obama's father's home country.

"How are you feeling, Anton?" his mom asked him.

She took his hand in hers, and he looked up at her. There were tears in her eyes, but a big smile on her face.

Even Officer Griggs looked like he'd been crying.

Anton thought about the last few days. Saturday morning, vandalizing the school; talking to Officer Griggs on the drive to the precinct; meeting Officer Harley, the first black cop in his precinct; meeting Paolo, who at the age of eighteen had taken part in such a historic election; hearing President Obama's speech.

Suddenly Anton knew what it all meant.

He used to believe a boy who came from his neighborhood — the ghetto, the projects — could never become anyone important in this world. But now, the stories he'd heard from all these people — even his own mother — had showed him that the world is an amazing place, and changing all the time.

"So, Anton?" Mom asked again. "How do you feel?"

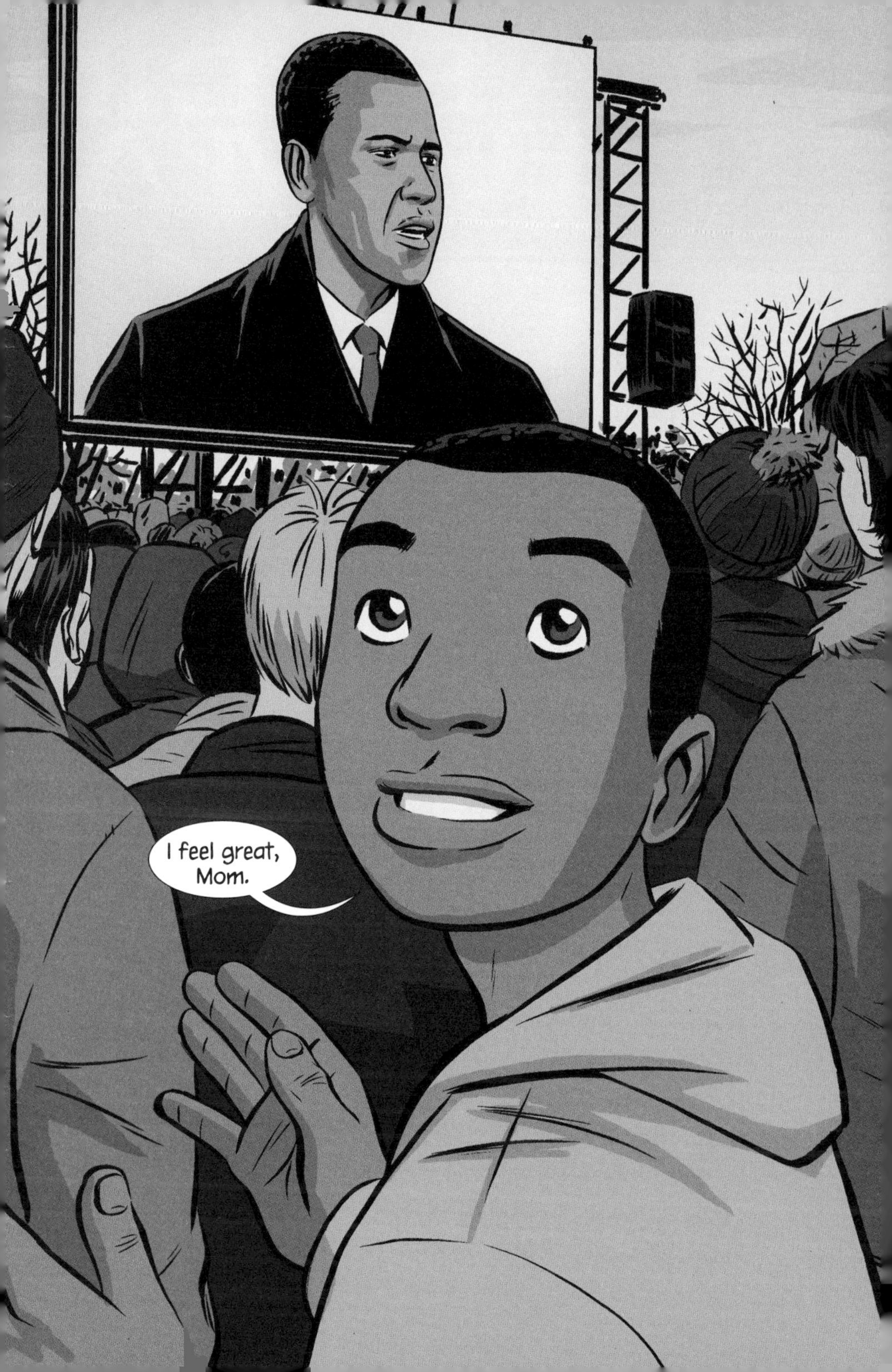
I feel great, Mom.

MORE ABOUT BARACK OBAMA

Barack Hussein Obama II was born August 4, 1961, in Honolulu, Hawaii. His mother was American, and his father was from Kenya, making Barack Obama the first African-American president.

President Obama's parents divorced when he was two. He spent most of his childhood in Hawaii. For many of those years, he lived with his grandparents. After high school, he moved to California, where he attended Occidental College. Two years later, he transferred to Columbia University in New York City. There, he studied political science and international relations. He graduated in 1983 with a B.A. in political science.

After working in New York and Chicago, Barack Obama entered law school at Harvard. He was selected editor of the prestigious *Harvard Law Review* at the end of his first year. He was the first African-American head of the *Harvard Law Review.*

In 1992, Barack married Michelle Robinson. The couple met when they were two of very few African-Americans at the Chicago law firm where they both worked.

Six years later, in 1998, the Obamas' first daughter, Malia, was born. Another daughter, Sasha, was born in 2001.

Barack Obama's political career began in 1996, when he was elected to the Illinois State Senate. He was reelected in 1998.

Though he was defeated in the primaries during his 2000 run for election to the U.S. House of Representatives, Barack decided to run for U.S. Senate in 2004. During the campaign, Obama was asked to deliver a keynote address at the 2004 Democratic Convention.

Obama was elected to the U.S. Senate in November 2004, making him the fifth African-American senator in United States history.

In 2007, Obama announced that he would run for U.S. President. He and his running mate, Joe Biden, won the election on November 4, 2008 against John McCain and his running mate, Sarah Palin.

Barack Obama was sworn in as the 44th President of the United States on January 4, 2009.

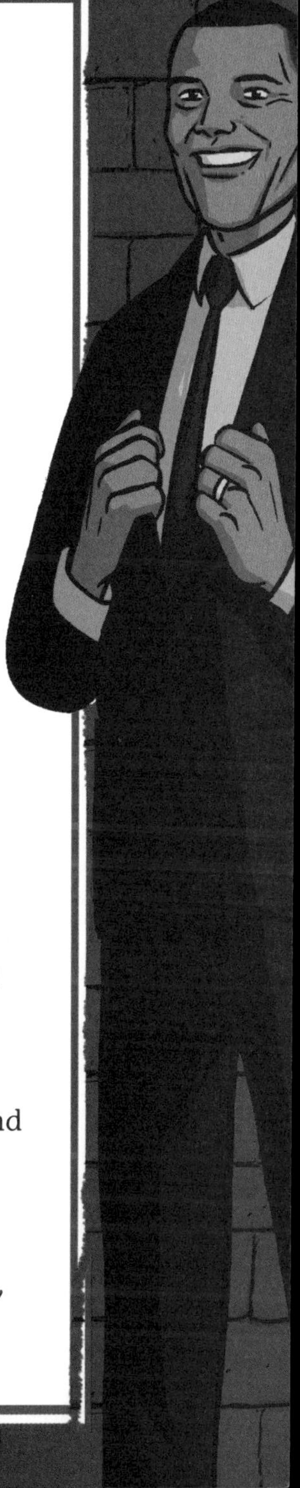

ABOUT THE AUTHOR

★ ★

Eric Stevens lives in St. Paul, Minnesota. He is studying to become a middle-school English teacher. Some of his favorite things include pizza, playing video games, watching cooking shows on TV, riding his bike, and trying new restaurants. Some of his least favorite things include olives and shoveling snow.

★ ★ ★ ★ ★ ★ ★ ★ ★ ★ ★ ★ ★ ★ ★ ★ ★ ★

GLOSSARY

★ ★

creed (KREED)—what a person believes

glee (GLEE)—enjoyment and delight

hypothermia (hye-puh-THUR-mee-uh)—suffering from very low body
temperature

inauguration (in-aw-gyuh-RAY-shuhn)—the ceremony of swearing in a public
official

intense (in-TENSS)—very strong; emotional

politician (pol-uh-TISH-uhn)—someone who runs for or holds a government
office

precinct (PREE-singkt)—a police station in an area or district in a city or town

segregation (seg-ruh-GAY-shuhn)—the act or practice of keeping people or
groups apart. Segregation of schools and public facilities along racial lines is
illegal in the United States.

suspense (suh-SPENSS)—an anxious and uncertain feeling caused by having to
wait to see what happens

vandalism (VAN-duhl-iz-uhm)—the act of needlessly damaging or destroying
other people's property

vapor (VAY-pur)—moisture in the air

★ ★

DISCUSSION QUESTIONS

★ ★

1. Why was Anton spray-painting the wall? What else could he have done to stop feeling so angry about school?

2. Talk about the people Anton met in this book. What did he learn from each of them?

3. Barack Obama was the first African-American person elected president. Why is that important? Who are some other "firsts" you can think of? Talk about it.

WRITING PROMPTS

★ ★

1. This story is historical fiction. That means that the historical event is true, but the characters and storyline are fictional. Choose a historical event and write your own story that takes place on that day.

2. What do you think happens after this book ends? Write a chapter that continues the story.

3. The inauguration made Anton feel great. How does the story make you feel? Write about your reactions to this book.

★ ★ ★ ★ ★ ★ ★ ★ ★ ★ ★ ★ ★ ★ ★ ★ ★ ★

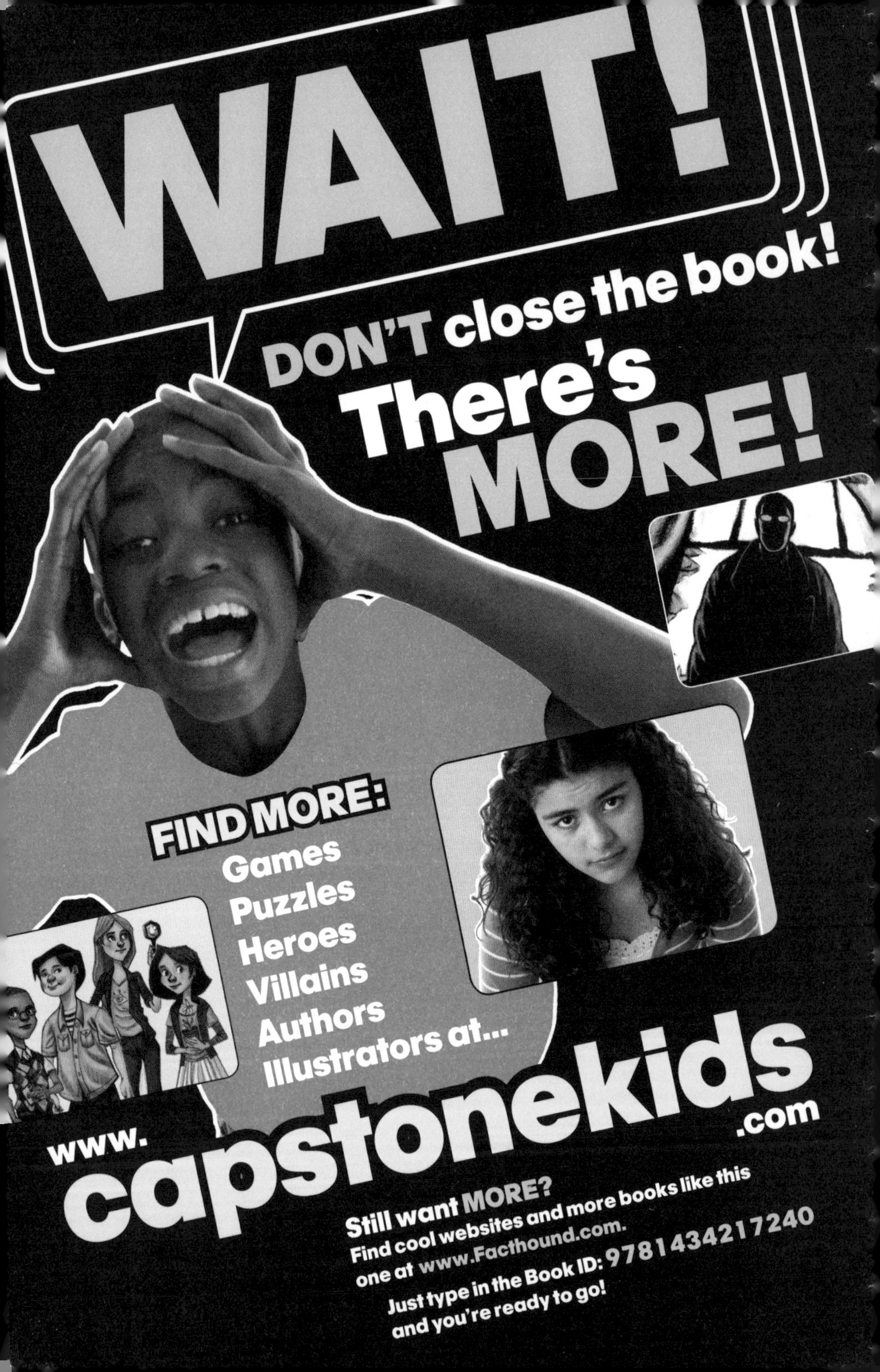
WAIT!
DON'T close the book!
There's MORE!
FIND MORE:
Games
Puzzles
Heroes
Villains
Authors
Illustrators at...
www.capstonekids.com
Still want MORE?
Find cool websites and more books like this one at www.Facthound.com.
Just type in the Book ID: 9781434217240
and you're ready to go!